"How can you not fall in love wit[...]
her own plane, combusts the bad guy[...]
and has a weakness for sexy men and deep-fried chicken?"*

PRAISE FOR
Charmed & Dangerous

"From assassination attempts to steamy sex scenes to the summoning of magical powers, Havens covers a lot of ground. Weaving together political intrigue, romance, and fantasy is definitely tricky, but Havens makes it work in this quick-paced, engaging story with unique and likable characters."   —*Booklist*

"Mix the mystique of all three Charlie's Angels, Buffy's brass and scrappy wit, add the globe-trotting smarts of Sydney Bristow, and you might come up with enough cool to fill Bronwyn's little witchy finger."   —*Britta Coleman,
author of *Potter Springs*

"A funny, imaginative take on what it would be like being a young, single, powerful witch."   —*Fresh Fiction*

"This is a refreshing, fast-paced entry for Havens, who pulls out all stops to put the world to rights with humor, some good old-fashioned street fighting—witch style—and some well-deserved romance."   —*Romantic Times*

continued . . .

Charmed & Ready

Candace Havens

BERKLEY BOOKS, NEW YORK

THE BERKLEY PUBLISHING GROUP
Published by the Penguin Group
Penguin Group (USA) Inc.
375 Hudson Street, New York, New York 10014, USA
Penguin Group (Canada), 90 Eglinton Avenue East, Suite 700, Toronto, Ontario M4P 2Y3, Canada
(a division of Pearson Penguin Canada Inc.)
Penguin Books Ltd., 80 Strand, London WC2R 0RL, England
Penguin Group Ireland, 25 St. Stephen's Green, Dublin 2, Ireland (a division of Penguin Books Ltd.)
Penguin Group (Australia), 250 Camberwell Road, Camberwell, Victoria 3124, Australia
(a division of Pearson Australia Group Pty. Ltd.)
Penguin Books India Pvt. Ltd., 11 Community Centre, Panchsheel Park, New Delhi—110 017, India
Penguin Group (NZ), Cnr. Airborne and Rosedale Roads, Albany, Auckland 1310, New Zealand
(a division of Pearson New Zealand Ltd.)
Penguin Books (South Africa) (Pty.) Ltd., 24 Sturdee Avenue, Rosebank, Johannesburg 2196,
South Africa

Penguin Books Ltd., Registered Offices: 80 Strand, London WC2R 0RL, England

This book is an original publication of The Berkley Publishing Group.

PRINTING HISTORY
Berkley trade paperback edition / September 2006

Library of Congress Cataloging-in-Publication Data

Havens, Candace, 1963–
    Charmed & ready / Candace Havens.—Berkley trade pbk. ed.
        p. cm.
    ISBN 0-425-21161-4
    1. Witches—Fiction. 2. Rock musicians—Fiction. I. Title. II. Title: Charmed and ready.

PS3608.A878C474 2006
813'.6—dc22

                                                                      2006042780

PRINTED IN THE UNITED STATES OF AMERICA

10 9 8 7 6 5 4 3 2 1

To all the divas of the world who love a great pair of shoes

Acknowledgments

A special thank-you to the lovely Anne Sowards for taking on my books and making the transition seamless. Leslie Gelbman and the rest of the gang at Berkley, thank you for making my dreams come true.

Sha-Shana Crichton, please know how much I admire your patience and intelligence. To the writers of DFW Writers' Workshop, NTRWA, FF&P, ChickLit, Romance Divas, Witchy Chicks, The Fast Draft crew, and all of you who have supported me, helped with research, and listened to countless drafts, thank you.

To the readers of *Charmed & Dangerous* who kept asking, "When does the next one come out?" Thank you.

Britta, Shannon, and Rosemary, your friendships are priceless. I tip my tiara to you all. Jodi Thomas, Jennifer Archer, Gena Showalter, Laurie Moore, and Sarah Clark Jordan, thank you for always being there when I have the "crazy" questions.

Steve, Jeff, and Parker, I love you all. Mom, Dad, and Grandma Irby and the rest of my family, you have always believed, and I am forever grateful.

Music is often my inspiration and these folks helped my story along: Sheryl Crow, Joss Stone, The Rolling Stones, U2, The Killers, Switchfoot, Yellowcard, Jack Johnson, Faith Hill, and Martina McBride.

Prologue

"Two weeks of sipping raspberry margaritas and mojitos on the beach. No worries, just sun and fun." I shifted on the dirt floor. The smell of dead rats overwhelmed my senses. I couldn't face Simone. The chains binding us to the steel pole wouldn't allow much movement.

"I know." The demon slayer sighed.

"I'm taking time off and we'll do nothing but fun girly things. Spa days, tanning, a trip to the hair salon to see Sir David; he's a master with highlights." I bit my lip and looked up at the ceiling. Nothing there that would help us.

"He is." The chains rattled. "And you're beautiful. Your hair's never looked better."

I ignored the compliment. "Sleep as much as you want."

"Well, there was that first day." Her voice carried an edge.

"I was shot with a tranquilizer dart." I tried to grab the chain with my hand, but was bound too tight.

"Yes, but you slept like a baby for twenty-four hours." She had the nerve to giggle.

"Get away from all of your troubles at home and experience how the Hollywood set lives. See the sights, and hang with the real *party crowd*," I grumbled. I couldn't help it.

"We were at a great party before this happened, and that one guy totally wanted in your pants."

"Yes, a demon who wanted to impregnate me with slime-filled eggs." I knocked on the pole with my fist. "This so sucks."

"Yep."

The door burst open. "Who is the first to die?" the demon roared. Stupid creep was way too dramatic. That's Hollywood for you.

I guess it was time.

"I'll go. Anything is better than listening to her bitch." Simone slid halfway up the pole.

"Simone?"

"What?"

The demon unshackled her chains. He smelled like dog pee. I suppose that was his natural aroma. At the party his body odor hadn't been so offensive. But he'd been masking as a human.

"If we get out of this, I'm going to kick your ass." No levity in my voice.

"You'll have to wait in line. And I'd like to remind you, the assholes waiting upstairs are after you."

I cleared my throat. Damn, I'd guessed they were warlocks. Simone's senses confirmed it. "True. I'm sorry. None of this is your fault." It really wasn't. I tend to get in a bad mood when doom is near. I couldn't keep the worry from my voice. "I didn't mean it, before. You know that, right?"

She half laughed. "I know, Bron. It's not your fault, either."

"Enough talk. Come, demon slayer. The master waits." His big horned head motioned my way. "I'm going to enjoy watching you squirm, witch."

Can't believe I thought that jerk was cute at the party. He pulled Simone up the stairway and I smelled the smoke from the fire as he opened the door.

Man, I hate it when bad guys sacrifice my friends. And I especially hate the fact I'm next.

One

Monday, 9 A.M.
Manhattan
Spells: 5
Charms: 3
Bad guys: 0 (Unless you count the almost boyfriend who ignores me)

I've finally discovered something I don't like about Sweet, Texas. August. I like warm weather but this is insane. I walked out the front door to get the paper, and by the time I returned to the porch, my body was covered in sweat.

Ack!

Stood under the vent in the living room for a good three minutes to cool off. I've got to pack for New York, which I understand isn't much cooler than Sweet right now.

The prime minister called last night and asked me to meet him there. He's one of my best clients, and the guy who gave me the big break in witchy protection. So, I usually do whatever he wants. And he's a good guy, who cares about his people.

"Bronwyn, I'm meeting with the vice president, Dr. Zocando, Sheik Azir and that rock star Zane. We're in talks about world hunger, and I'd like you to sit in with us." The PM's usually clipped tones sounded a bit frantic.

"Is everything okay, sir?"

"Miles is on vacation and things don't seem to run well when he's not around."

The PM's snippy twit of an assistant, Miles, was a royal bore and pain. But he did keep the diplomat's schedule running smooth.

"Wait. Did you say Sheik Azir would be there?"

"Yes, is that a problem?"

"No, sir. I just wasn't sure I'd heard you correctly." I'd had an almost romance with the sheik a few months ago, and hadn't seen or heard from him since. Didn't really have time to think much about seeing him again, but I suddenly felt queasy.

"I'll be there around 8 P.M. Will that work?"

"Yes, we have a room booked for you at the Gansevoort Hotel."

"Oh, before you go. Is there anything in particular you want me to look for at the meeting?"

"I'll explain when you get here." No good-bye, he just hung up the phone.

Well, if I'm going to make lunch with Sam before I leave, I'd better hurry up.

12 A.M.

Lunch with Sam. Dinner with Azir. It's been one hell of a strange day.

Met Sam for lunch at Lulu's in the middle of his first day back at work. He sat at a booth and had iced tea waiting for me.

I love Lulu's. It smells like fresh bread, carrot cake and hamburgers. Ms. Johnnie and Ms. Helen, who run the café, have lived a lot of life, and are some of the best cooks I've ever known.

Sam wore jeans and a blue and white striped button-down. You could take the prep out of Harvard, but couldn't get the Harvard out of the prep. He'd only recently traded his khakis for jeans. I thought it a great accomplishment—mostly because his ass looks really good in a pair of button-fly Levi's.

Every time I see him, my heart does that funny flutter thing. I've never been in love like this, and it's still kind of weird for me. In a good way.

I kissed Sam and touched his cheek. He looked sallow and tired around his beautiful blue eyes. The fact that he suffered made me want to kill that warlock who had attacked him all over again.

I knew better than to ask him how he felt. Two months ago when he opened his eyes after days in a coma, he made me promise to never ask that question. He pushed himself so hard in physical therapy that he proved the surgeons who said he wouldn't be able to walk for at least a year wrong.

Sam used a cane, propped next to him in the booth, but he walked just fine.

"So how is the first day back at work?" I poured sugar into my tea and gave it a stir.

"Hectic, but great." His smile still made my stomach flip-flop. "Lots of heat rash and sunburn for the most part. So it hasn't been that difficult of a day. I'm still not used to being on my feet so much. But it's all good."

Ms. Johnnie, who looked adorable in strawberry colored Capri pants and matching T-shirt, stopped by to take our order. Rumor had it that she would be turning seventy in a few months, but you'd never know it by the way she dressed and hopped around the restaurant like an athlete on steroids.

We agreed on turkey sandwiches and vinegar chips. Nothing too heavy for hot days like this.

"Um." I picked at the corners of my paper napkin. "I need to tell you something and I think it best if I just come out and say it."

"Okay." He frowned.

"I've got to fly to New York tonight."

"Okay, and this is bad because?"

"Well, it's my first time to leave Sweet since—" I blew out a breath.

"The accident?" He added.

"Yes, and well, the prime minister called and asked if I would please come, and I've turned down the last few jobs."

"What do you mean, you turned down jobs? I never asked you to do any such thing. Bronywn, what's going on?"

"Well, you were so sick and I couldn't leave. And I love you," I said in a rush. "Wait, that came out wrong. I love you and I didn't want to be away. Not because you were sick, but because I love you. Crap."

I'm so bad at this man thing. Just the worst.

He chuckled.

"I think I understand, and I appreciate all of your tender loving care the past few months. There were many days when I'm not certain I could have made it without you, but I never meant for you to give up your job to help me out. I love you too." He took my hand.

His touch always reassures me. I love the strength of him. The kindness of his soul has touched me since the day we met.

I squeezed his fingers. "I know."

"You said the prime minister would be there. Who else?"

I swallowed. "Oh, you know. The regular dignitaries, that musician Zane. People like that."

"Will Azir be there?" There was a hint of an edge in his voice.

I'd been staring with great intent at his hand holding mine and I raised my eyes to meet his.

"Yes."

"And you were nervous about telling me?"

"A little."

"He's your friend, and he's in love with you. I can't say it doesn't bother me, but I can live with it if you can." He let go of my hand and looked at his watch.

"I've got to get back to the office." He pushed himself up with one hand on the table and grabbed the cane.

I stood and kissed him. "Sam," I whispered against his lips.

"It really is okay, Bron. I just need to go. And so do you. It's time for you to go. What we have is real and we both have to learn to trust it. I'll be here when you come back."

"I'll call you when I get to New York."

I started to walk away and he grabbed my hand. Pulling me tight to his chest, he kissed me so hard that, eight hours later, I can still feel the imprint of his lips.

See, that's the thing with Sam. He sticks with me more than anyone I've ever met. I handed my heart to him a few months ago, and it's been the scariest, most wonderful thing I ever did.

Had I known when the prime minister invited me to dinner tonight that Azir would be there, I think I would have passed.

I hadn't been ready to see him again. Oh, the meal went well.

We all chatted about world affairs and who would be there the next day. The prime minister believes that this Zane guy is going to bring a great deal of attention to the cause.

We were in the VIP section of the restaurant, on the second level. The couples downstairs celebrated anniversaries and birthdays over candlelit dinners with the cream-colored tablecloths, and bottles of champagne in neat silver cylinders.

But everything seemed so weird. I'm not sure what I expected. Maybe for Azir to give me longing looks throughout the meal. I couldn't keep from sneaking glances every once in a while. He was dressed in Hugo Boss pinstripes.

His dark brown eyes, framed with those deadly long lashes, barely registered my presence. And he gave no indication that he had any interest in me at all. Well, in *that* way.

Strictly professional.

I guess that's a good thing, since I'm with Sam now.

I'd dressed up for dinner in a long black skirt, four-inch Manolos Mom gave me and a red wrap top. I reasoned that I wanted to look nice because of the strict dress code of the five-star restaurant. But in some twisted, womanly way, I also wanted to impress the sheik.

There. I said it. I wanted him to notice me.

That's just sick.

Two months ago he told me he loved me. Then he left town, and I hadn't heard a peep since. And I thought, "Good riddance." I didn't need the complication.

And then tonight when he didn't really seem to notice me, my ego deflated. I have to stop. I'm not going through all of that again.

He wants to keep things on a professional level, and I should be grateful.

But at the end of the night, when I shook his hand, the sparks flew between us. Just for an instant when we touched he looked in my eyes, and I was lost. He smelled like sandalwood.

No, Bronwyn. Bad girl.

Azir bad. Sam good.

Easy peasy. No need to get all crazy again.

Take a big breath, old girl, and just get over yourself.

He's moved on. I've moved on.

Crap, who would knock on the door at this hour?

I sent my mind past the wards to take a peek.

Azir?

Two

5 P.M.
Manhattan
Potions: 3
Charms: 3
Spells: 5
Sexy rock stars: 1

I've spent the last few hours putting wards on everyone's rooms. The Gansevoort Hotel is a small boutique hotel, which is good for our purposes. The less people around, the better.

It isn't my style, but I love the sleek modern look of the rooms with their big plasma televisions.

Also gave Azir and the prime minister new charms laced with primrose. In the old days primrose was used to keep the fairies out of the house. With a decent spell it works well against all evil.

Ack. My brain hurts. Too much information and I'm in over-load. It doesn't help that Azir is playing some kind of mind game and he didn't mention the rules.

He stopped by last night to drop off the files the prime minis-ter forgot to give me at dinner. Turns out, Azir's suite is just across from mine.

Interesting. Have no idea if he set it up that way.

"Here's the file on the participants of the meeting tomorrow morning." He'd loosened his tie and shirt. His dark chest hair peeked through.

I had a sudden urge to reach up and touch him to feel the curly softness for myself. But I resisted.

"Thanks." I took the folder and leafed through a couple of pages.

"Well, good night then." He turned to step across the hall.

"Azir?"

He stopped and turned around.

"Yes."

"Is there a reason you've decided to treat me like the black plague? You didn't say two words to me directly at dinner and you seem—I don't know. Uptight?"

He frowned. "I can assure you I am not uptight. This meeting tomorrow morning is important to me and I have a lot on my mind." He pushed through his doorway and never looked back.

Whatever. Maybe he needs some distance between us, or he might not give a damn anymore. It's kind of stupid, because Sam's my man, but it's weird to see Azir acting this way.

I didn't have much time to worry. The prime minister wanted me at breakfast early the next morning.

That's where I meet rock star extraordinaire Zane. I knew his music. Crap, you'd have to live on Mercury not to have heard him. He's everywhere.

Before I read his file I suspected that he used this World Hunger Organization as a PR ploy. But he's really a pretty straight-up guy. He's donated millions of his own funds and set up five different benefit concerts to raise money for the hungry children of the world.

"He's brought more attention to the issue of hunger in the last year, than we have in the last twenty," the PM explained before Zane joined us for breakfast. "He has a great passion for the work." The PM buttered a roll. "Ah, here he is."

I'd seen pictures several times but they didn't do the man justice. He wore a white poet's shirt with ruffled sleeves and black leather pants that would have looked idiotic on anyone else. On him it worked.

His golden curls were professionally mussed and his green eyes took in the room as he crossed the floor. He owned it. The whole place, as soon as he entered. I'd never seen such a presence.

"Prime Minister." Zane held his hand out to grasp the PM's. "So good to see you again. How's your tennis game?"

"Better. We should set up a match soon." The PM smiled. "I think I might make you work a bit harder the next time you beat me."

Zane laughed. "Well, you can certainly hope that will be the case."

It was difficult to reconcile this rock star, whose life had been tabloid fodder for the past five years, with a man who played tennis with world leaders and helped care for the poor.

His penchant for wooing the fairer sex had been news on the

entertainment shows for years. And I wondered as I watched him if any of it was true.

He turned to me, took a step back and put his hand on his heart. "And who is this gorgeous beauty?"

I shook my head and snorted, because that's what cool chicks do.

The PM looked at me curiously, as if beauty was an odd word in relation to me, and then he introduced me. "This is Bronwyn, a consultant friend of mine."

The PM was up-front about my chosen profession. Consultant actually covered a multitude of sins, and no one ever asked what I consulted about.

Zane stuck out his hand and I did the same. When he touched me, my body relaxed. As if I'd been comforted by a close friend, which was strange since I don't know him.

Maybe that's what he used to get all those women into bed. He wasn't a warlock, but he definitely had special abilities.

"Charmed to meet you, lovely woman, and so happy you could join us for breakfast." He sat down with a great flourish and propped his elbows on the table.

He and the PM talked about a new project proposal directed at international corporations that would underwrite the cost of feeding a large portion of the Third World.

Halfway through the conversation Zane stopped talking and turned to me again. "Bronwyn?"

"Yes?"

"Are you Simone's friend? She's a demon slayer in L.A."

Hello sudden shift in conversation. What was this about? "I do know Simone. How do you know her?" Most people in the "real world" know Simone as a scientist and professor, not as a slayer.

He waved a hand. "Oh we've been friends for ages. She called you once when I was at her place. Something about a demon she needed to kill. She told me that you are a powerful—um. Oh." His eyes widened and he looked to the prime minister.

"A powerful witch? Yes, she is." The PM smiled.

"Wow." He reached out and grabbed my hand. "I've wanted to meet you since that day. Simone isn't impressed by much, so when she turned to you for help I knew you must be special."

"Well, thanks." I shrugged, not really knowing what to say. It was kind of sweet, and the word "special" isn't usually spoken by Simone.

Realizing he must sound like one of those crazed fans he's always running away from, he grinned sheepishly. "Sorry. It just dawned on me who you were."

"No worries." I forked up some eggs.

And he returned to his conversation with the PM.

I had a chance to call Simone later and she had all kinds of helpful information. Well, not helpful really, but interesting just the same.

"Oh, that Zane, he's a hot one. Did he try to get into your pants yet?"

"No, don't be stupid." Should he have? Damn, have I lost my touch? And why would I want him to? "Simone, you know I'm with Sam."

"Just because you're with someone doesn't mean you're dead. And that Zane is a pro at making a woman feel very much alive." Simone always has such a direct way of putting things.

"Whenever he's in town he calls and says, "Hello, luv, how about a bit of a tuck in?" Simone's British accent was lacking, but it made me laugh.

"I tell him to come on over baby, and tuck it in wherever you want."

Oh my God. "Well, he's not tucking in anything here. But I did think he was an interesting guy and he asked me out for dinner."

"I'd say skip the food and move on to the fun. But I know, I know, *you're with Sam.*"

"Yes, I *am.*"

"Zane's smart, Bronwyn, and you know that's something I don't care much about where men are concerned. The dumber the better when it comes to a good fuck. But the guy is brilliant. Even if you don't do the nasty you'll have a great time. And when are you coming out to see me? It's been ages since you've been here." Simone cleared her throat.

"I'll think about it. Kind of busy the next few weeks with different assignments, but we'll see."

I could hear her running down the street. "Hey!" she yelled. "Simone?"

"Gotta go. Asshole Nako demon is trying to eat a baby."

Click and she was gone. She's never happy unless she's had a good kill.

Now I've got two hours to get ready. And I need to go online and make a donation to the World Hunger Organization. After listening to all of the statistics about starving children, I had a tremendous sense of guilt. I'm donating my exorbitant fee for helping the prime minister. It only seems fair. I'm making enough to feed a small village for a year, maybe two.

Argh. Don't want to think about it.

What am I going to wear to dinner? I want to look good, but not hey-come-jump-in-my-pants good. Hmm.

I A.M.

So tired.

Zane wore me out.

Simone's right. He's a fantastic man.

I don't know if Azir and the PM invited themselves to dinner or if Zane asked them, but we all ended up sharing a table at Banats. It's one of those places where the waiters are grumpy but the food is great.

We sat on the first floor at a table in the back, surrounded by security for the PM, Azir and Zane. I don't know how they found this table on a Friday night, but money and power talk.

When Azir and the prime minister walked over to a different table to greet a friend, Zane whispered in my ear, "So, how long has the sheik been hot for you?"

I swallowed my Pellegrino wrong and choked.

He patted me on the back and laughed. "So, I take it you've known for a while."

My instinct was to lie, but he would see through it. "Yes, I've known for a couple of months. But I'm with someone else."

"Oh, so it's a one-sided lust."

I puckered my lips. "Well, not really. I like him a lot too, but not in the same way. I'm with someone special. It's just very complicated. Hey, he hasn't said anything to me tonight. How did you know?"

He leaned back in his chair. "Oh, my beauty. When a man ignores a woman like you, it's because he can't control himself. If he lets his guard down . . . Well, it's just tough on a gent like him. All strong and he-mannish. The poor man's ego must be in the loo."

I laughed. Azir, the he-man. It fit.

After that, Zane controlled the conversation, bringing Azir in and talking about everything from global warming to jazz music. He made a really uncomfortable situation bearable.

"Well gents, it's been a wonderful evening but I've promised this lovely woman a night of dancing so we're off." He pulled me from the table and out the door.

"Dancing?" I sat next to him in the limo. "When did we mention dancing? And did you see Azir's face?"

"Priceless, my dove. Absolutely priceless. If he could have sliced me in two with that look, he would have. But I had a bit of inspiration at the table and decided we needed to work off our troubles with a twirl on the dance floor.

"I don't know about you but my brain could use a bit of a rest from all of the seriousness of the world." He reached forward and tapped on the window. "Can you drop us at Vice, good man?"

Vice. Oh, man. What a place. Everyone from S and M enthusiasts to the young, hot celebs of the day showed up there. We skipped the line around the block and were ushered in the back entrance.

Even though it was more private, Zane was stopped several times to sign autographs.

"Sorry, luv," he said as he guided me into the VIP lounge. Everything was black except for the lavender lighting. Very surreal.

Most of the people in that part of the club were much too cool to be impressed by one of the biggest rock stars in the world. So, we spent the next few hours downing cocktails and dancing.

Have you ever thought about how easy it is to get drunk when you dance? You're always so thirsty. The club was hot and I don't mean the temperature.

I tried not to stare at the woman without a shirt who had her nipples triple pierced. I still don't know what that guy had in his lip; it looked like a small saucer. But if the saucer didn't turn you on, the huge erection poking through his mesh shorts might have.

It was wild, but Zane and I ended the night the best of friends. He never once tried anything, and I, surprisingly, wasn't disappointed.

I don't know. Maybe I'm not his type, but it didn't matter. I'm mixing us both a hangover potion for the morning. We'll need it before the big meeting.

Three

Noon

Potions: 2

Spells: 1

Bad guys: 1 (But I can't find him)

Some days the toughest part of my job is staying awake. I'm in meetings with some of the most important people in the world, decision makers, diplomats, politicians—and all I can think about is not yawning.

Man, I don't know if it was all the dancing, the hangover or what, but I could barely keep my eyes open. Well, that was before the Big Message.

They must die.

That's what I heard in my head. I was doodling on a piece of paper in the conference room when all of a sudden someone penetrated my mental shield. The message was so loud I jumped out of my chair and made a complete ass out of myself.

When I bent down to pick up my pad and paper I heard it again. Almost like a chant.

There weren't any other magical folks in the room and it was a small crowd of about twenty dignitaries. It was one of those meetings-before-the-big-summit things. The PM asked me to sit in just to get a feel for the room. And until I heard the death threat, it had been a pretty positive vibe.

My mind swept the room to see if I could pinpoint who had thought those words, but I couldn't feel anything at first. I did quick tiny probes into each participant, and discovered I wasn't the only one who was ready for lunch.

Had I imagined it?

I don't think so. And it's possible it may have come from somewhere besides the room.

After the meeting I was more than a little distracted, but the PM insisted on introducing me to Dr. Zocando. He's been doing humanitarian work in Africa for longer than I can remember.

"Doctor, this is Bronwyn, the young woman I was telling you about." The PM gestured toward me.

I reached out a hand to shake, but the doc bowed. I inclined my head.

He was a tall man, at least six three, with the stature and grace of royalty. It's appropriate since most of the world sees him that way. My brother, Brett, works as a doctor in Africa on an AIDS initiative, and he thinks Zocando is some kind of hero. And Brett doesn't like anyone.

Zocando's expression turned serious. "The prime minister tells me that you saved his life on more than one occasion. This is most impressive."

Aw shucks, the PM's been bragging again. That's so sweet. "Thank you, sir."

"I wonder if perhaps I might consult with you at a later date. We have some security concerns that . . ." He eyed someone behind me. "Well, this isn't the time to discuss such matters. Prime Minister, Bronwyn. I bid you a good day."

I turned to see who had entered the room. It was Azir. Interesting. The weird thing was, I got a strange vibe from the doc. Like something was off. And he'd been protected by some kind of mental shield because when I tried to sweep his mind, I didn't see a thing.

Odd that he would consult me about anything. I don't think he likes women much. Don't know why, just a feeling.

Oh, I need to call Sam. I want to see how he's doing his first week back at the office.

7 P.M.

Confused witches: I

Okay, so like Azir's been ignoring me big time. I get it. But why, oh why, did he just ask me out to dinner? And what the hell am I going to tell Sam?

Azir called about an hour ago and asked if I could meet him and Zane downstairs around eight tonight. He would have known if I had plans or not, so I couldn't lie and tell him otherwise. Cool and nonchalant, I said, "Sure." Argh! Why did I do that? And I got the feeling last night that Azir didn't care at all for Zane.

Oh boy, this is going to be sooooo much fun.

I talked to Sam a few minutes earlier. He sounded tired.

"Hey baby, how was day two?" I said when he called me back.

He sighed and blew out a big breath. I could almost see him raking a hand through that gorgeous black hair of his. He'd let it grow out the last few months and it almost touches his collar.

"Good. Long day, but at least it went by quick. How about you?"

"Long day, but it didn't go by quite as fast as yours. I need to remember to take some herbals with me to keep me awake during these meetings."

"Were you out late last night?" It seemed a harmless question.

"Sort of. Had dinner with the PM and some other folks." I opened up my laptop while we chatted and checked my e-mail.

"Would one of those other folks have been Azir?" His voice didn't sound judgmental, more curious than anything.

"Well, he showed up. Yes." I didn't know what to say.

"How about Zane the rock star, was he there?" Now I did hear something in his voice. Annoyance.

"Yes, I believe he was," I hedged. I wasn't sure what Sam was thinking.

"Did you have fun dancing?"

Big pause. Then I coughed.

"Excuse me?" I finally got my voice back.

"With Zane, did you enjoy the Vice club? I'm just wondering because they have you looking pretty cozy holding hands and all, on *Entertainment Tonight*."

"What?" I coughed again, this time for real and flipped on the television.

"Margie called and told me to turn on the television, that she was watching you on *ET*. And sure enough there you were, holding hands with one of the biggest rock stars on the planet. Looking very cozy I might add, as you climbed in the back of a limo."

God, I'd been so drunk I hadn't even noticed the cameras.

"Oh, wow. I had no idea. Truth is we went dancing, I had too much to drink, I think Zane did too, and we were probably holding each other up. I pinky swear, Sam, there's nothing more than that going on." I don't know why I felt so defensive. But I could just imagine what he must be thinking. The fact that I was within a ten-mile radius of Azir was bad enough without this.

Sam sighed again. "I trust you, Bron. I have to, or this is never going to work. But do me a favor in the future and try to stay out of the media. I realize my reasons are selfish, but I'm not looking forward to rounds at the nursing home tomorrow. You're going to be the big buzz, and I'll have to explain that no, you aren't Zane's latest conquest, that we really are happy together."

"I am sorry, Sam. It's just—I'm sorry. I feel so stupid that I've let you down."

"I'm not bringing this up to make you feel bad, I just want you to know how it seems from the outside looking in."

We talked for a while longer and when we hung up it felt like everything was okay. I don't like to say it, but Sam's still fragile in some ways. I never want to hurt him, certainly not on purpose.

This whole relationship thing is tough for me. No, that's not what I mean. I mean it's difficult for me to remember that my actions can affect another person. I'm so used to going off on my own and doing whatever, but now someone else's feelings are involved, and I have to take that into consideration.

Which begs the question: Why in the hell did I just tell Azir I'd have dinner with him and Zane?

So stupid.

8 A.M.

Guilt-free witches: 1

Call me chicken, I don't care, but last night I ended up having room service and watching reruns of *Alias*. God, I love that show, I can't believe they cancelled it. I'd kill to have Jennifer Garner's legs. They are a petite girl's dream.

And I've got to get Simone to teach me some more martial arts moves. That Sydney Bristow can kick some ass.

So, I'm only admitting it here, but I totally lied last night and told Azir that I wasn't feeling well. A migraine. I get them sometimes, especially when I'm trying to do too many mental readings or magic at once.

Thankfully, he wasn't in his room when I called so I left a message for him, and just in case, I left a message with Zane's assistant, Georgette.

Coward that I am, I holed up in my room and watched TV and played Texas Hold 'Em on the computer. Which got me to thinking how fun would it be to get all these dignitaries together for a game of cards. I bet they'd all be champs at bluffing.

I found out the guys had planned to go to some gallery opening, which I'm sure would be covered by the press. The last thing I needed to do was show up with Azir on one arm and Zane on the other. It would have probably killed poor Sam.

I called him around ten to tell him good night. Even though it was only nine there in Sweet, he sounded like I woke him up.

"Bron?" He whispered.

"Yes, did I wake you?"

"Hmmm. I must have dozed off in front of the television again. I was watching *Alias* and the next thing I knew the phone rang."

Can I tell you how much I love this guy? He loves the show just as much as I do, but I have a feeling it's more for her sexy outfits and push-up bras than her ability to slay bad guys with a single kick.

"I didn't expect to hear from you again tonight."

"Well, I was sitting here missing you and I thought I'd just ring and say good night." I smiled. I did miss him so much. He has a way of brushing my hair off my forehead or holding my hand and rubbing his thumb across my knuckles, that makes me feel treasured. It sounds corny, but I love him so damn much.

"I miss you too, baby. I know you hate when I ask, but any idea when you might be coming home?" He yawned.

"Don't be silly. I don't hate when you ask that, but I don't have an answer. I hope we'll be done by the weekend. You know I'm going to jump your bones as soon as I hop out of that jet."

He laughed. "Good. I could do with a bit of bone jumping. Oh, I checked on Casper. Her pet door keeps getting stuck, so I left her in the house for tonight. Is that okay?"

The last few months my protector of a cat and supposed witch's familiar had been noticeably absent. When I lived in Manhattan, London and Paris, she never left my apartment or my side when we were home. Guess she feels like we are safer in Texas.

"She'll be fine. Her boyfriends in the neighborhood might not be happy, but they'll get over it."

That made him laugh.

"Well, I'll let you get some rest. I love you, Sam. Sleep well."

"I love you too. Don't go looking for trouble," he warned, but his tone was playful.

Now that made me laugh, because trouble almost always finds me.

1 A.M.
Someone just knocked on the door, but by the time I got to it no one was there. Weird.

I put a new ward on the door to keep the unwanted out. Now back to those sexy, sexy dreams involving Sam and a bottle of Hershey's syrup. I love making a sundae out of that man.

Four

Saturday, 10 A.M.
La Guardia tarmac
Spells: 5
Tired, traveling witches: 1
Dead guys: 1 (Dammit. Should have killed them all.)

*L*ast night is a bit of a blur.

We ended the meetings on Friday, and from what I could tell everything was copasetic. Everyone cooperated, there were even policy changes enforced and each country promised to donate large amounts of food and funds. All in all, very productive.

And I hadn't heard any more weird messages about someone wanting to kill people.

So last night, Zane had everybody who stayed in town to a club for a private concert. My God, that man is hot. I mean it. I swear, even some of the straight guys were drooling.

Anyway, he sang a couple of tunes and then let the house band keep the party going. There was great food and drinks flowed freely. Fun, fun, after a tough week.

I planned to head home, but the prime minister asked me to stay on at least one more day. He had something important he wanted to talk to me about.

After the debacle with Zane the other night, I wasn't sure I should go. But Zane begged and I'm a wuss, so there I sat.

He wore a yellow velvet suit with no shirt underneath. He should have looked like a chicken, but it was so tight and sexy. I don't know many men who could get away with that sort of thing.

I'd forgotten how mesmerizing his voice could be, especially in a live performance. After he finished singing, he came to the table where the prime minister and I sat.

"Well, luv, having a good time?"

I raised my glass to him. Diet Coke and bourbon, the best thing ever for tight shoulders and a tough week. That's not true, sex is the best thing. Bourbon is a close second. "I am, thank you. I like your suit."

He laughed. "What, this old thing?"

I rolled my eyes, and wondered what his zillion-dollar designer would say about that.

"Bronwyn, Zane has something he'd like to discuss with you." The prime minister came to the club in casual attire. Well, casual for him. A black pinstripe Armani, with a blue shirt. But he didn't have a tie on. I tried to think back and remember if I'd ever seen him without a tie in public. Nope. I'd seen him without a shirt once after he'd been poisoned and I had to heal him, but we were in the privacy of his hotel room at the time. He kind of reminds me of Hugh Grant, but so much more stuffy.

I turned my attention to the rock star. And in that moment the confidence fell from his face.

"What is it?" I urged.

Zane stared at his kicky little boots for a full minute. "I think someone is trying to kill me."

"Oh. Okay. Any ideas about the culprits?" I couldn't keep my eyebrow from going up. If he and the prime minister were playing games, this wasn't a fun one.

"Not beyond the usual suspects." He took a deep breath and shook the tension from his body. "In my business, stalkers are common and every drunk wanker thinks he can sing better. But this . . . Well, seems a bit more intense."

"In what way?" I shifted in my seat. My senses were on alert, scanning the club as he spoke. This was serious. I wish these idiots would tell me right away when someone is trying to kill them. At least as a common courtesy in case I got caught in the crossfire.

"There was a bomb found under his limousine last night," the prime minister spoke up. I'd been traveling with Zane just a few days before, and this was not welcome news.

"I swear I would have said something before," Zane twisted to look behind him, "but I had no idea that it was this serious."

"Maybe you should go back to the beginning," I interjected.

"Well, about a month ago there was a man with a gun outside my house in London. One of my security guards noticed him hanging out on the corner and called the cops. He told them that he'd only been waiting for a friend. Other than the fact that he had a gun, the police had no reason to hold him. Two days later the security guard was found dead in his flat. Strangled."

His frown deepened. "The police didn't think the two incidents were related, but I'm not so sure.

"Then last night." He shook his head. "Before we headed back to the hotel, Azir's people did a sweep of the car. That's when they found the bomb."

We weren't speaking, but since he is under my protection it might have been nice if the sheik could have mentioned this.

"But if it was on a car you shared, then it could have been for you or Azir." I held up a hand. "Of course, that isn't good news either way. But you don't know it was for you."

"No, you don't understand. My assistant, Georgette, had hired the car. It was under her name. Azir had come to the dinner in a separate car. It was only at the last minute that we decided to share mine."

"Okay, so are those the only two incidents?" I drummed my fingers on my leg.

"I've been thinking back today. There's been some odd people at the benefits we've been doing. They wear cloaks and weird contacts—their eyes sort of glow. I thought they must be some kind of cult that just wants to rock on, but I'm not so sure now. The security officers mentioned in the report that a weird chant was coming from the group."

I knew about weird cults, but this sounded more like warlocks to me. I've spent way too much time in bad warlocks' company. Chanting is something they love to do. It's how they bring forth the evil that follows.

I should probably say that there are thousands of do-gooding warlocks who would never hurt a fly. Sam is one of them. But most of the ones I come into contact with are assholes.

"Has anything strange happened at the concerts?"

"We've had a lot of people get sick. At first everyone believed it was food poisoning, but that was never proven. A couple of people had to be taken to the hospital."

The band interrupted with a loud guitar solo and Zane paused in his story. We all clapped for the guy when he finished and then Zane continued.

"And to be honest all of a sudden I have stage fright. I've never experienced anything like it before. But now it's almost debilitating. The prime minister seems to think I may have been cursed. I've been working through it, but every time I perform it gets tougher." He rubbed his hand over his tight stomach.

I did a quick aura check but didn't see anything dark and gloomy hanging over him. There were no holes, but his aura was a strange color—amber with brown dots. The dots might have something to do with his stage fright.

"When we get back to the hotel, I have some stuff in my bag that may help." I patted his arm in a comforting way. Onstage he had seemed so confident and rock god-ish that it was hard to believe he was frightened of anything.

"What kind of stuff? Like witch's brew?" He smiled.

I laughed. "Exactly like that, but a bit more tasty than you might imagine. Do you think perhaps this cult or whatever may be at the source of your troubles the last month?"

"I honestly don't know, but it's the only logical explanation. Like I said before, these aren't your garden variety stalkers, I have a feeling things are going to get a lot worse before they get better."

I had to agree. If he had a gang of warlocks against him, it only meant big trouble. I'd sensed a kind of power in Zane when

I first met him. I wondered if perhaps the warlocks wanted some part, if not all, of that power.

"What exactly was it that you wanted to ask me?"

Zane hesitated and then looked at the prime minister as he spoke. "We were wondering if you'd come back to London with us to see if you could help."

I gave the PM an evil look. He knew I needed to return home to Sam. I was worried about being gone for this long. I know he's so much better than he was a few months ago, but until he is one hundred percent, well . . .

"Bronwyn, I know you have commitments." The PM spoke with authority. "But I'm asking as a client and as a friend for you to help Zane."

He knew I wouldn't say no. The mention of us being friends had been kind of a low blow. I'm loyal. It's one of my best—and worst—character traits. I've put myself in harm's way more than once, out of loyalty to a friend.

Sam would have to go it alone a few more days. Maybe I could get Kira and Caleb to check on him.

"I'll come to England with you, but I can't stay for long. We'll try to get at the source as quickly as possible and deal with this."

I held up a hand again. "With one condition. You have to do exactly what I tell you. If we're dealing with what I think we are, this is more dangerous than either of you could imagine. These people do mean harm. They aren't just some crazy cult."

Zane shrugged. "No problem. I'll do whatever you ask. Consider me under your spell." He wiggled an eyebrow.

Please, but he was funny. Any guy who can find humor in a situation this dire gets a plus-one in my book.

When we were leaving the club I discovered he hadn't exaggerated at all.

The limo pulled up, and five characters in cloaks jumped from the shadows. I could feel the magic roll off of a few of them. The others were just there for the fun of it. They surrounded the car. I could see why Zane had been frightened.

With the black cloaks covering them, all that showed were their orange glowing eyes.

"She's a witch!" The largest of the warlocks yelled. As he did so, he threw a small fireball at me. I didn't have time to roll my eyes, but I so wanted to.

I don't understand why warlocks are so fucking stupid. They always underestimate the power of their opponents. Especially if said opponent is a woman.

I caught the fireball in my hand. See, that's my power. I'm good with fire and blowing things up. Since I couldn't see the warlock's expression, I had no idea what he thought about my trick. But the two men who didn't have magic made a run for it. Smart humans.

The other three stood together in front of the car and began a chant. Some Latin crap about binding my powers. I tossed the fireball at them and then flicked a small burn to their shoes, or at least where I thought their feet might be. With all of that fabric, who could tell?

The two on the outside did a tippy-toe dance and yelled, "Hot, hot, hot." If I hadn't been so pissed it would have been kind of funny.

The one in the middle didn't move. He either could control the burn, or he was more powerful than I'd suspected. I doubted the second one. He might be more talented but he was definitely not much in the way of power.

Then he spoke. "He is ours, witch. He's been given to us by our master. You cannot protect him."

His voice sounded familiar. Eerily so, but I couldn't place it. A shiver ran down my back, and I shook it off. I put my hands on my hips. "Look, I'm trying to be nice and not kill you, but if you want to live you have to tell me what I want to know. Then turn yourself over to the spook squad."

He pointed a finger at Zane. "You cannot save him. His soul is ours." With that he threw his cloak in front of his face as if he were about to disappear. No way was this jerk getting away.

I tossed a larger fireball, twice the size of the one before, and it hit right in the center of his hood. Poof! Seconds later all that was in the spot were ashes.

I turned to the PM and Zane, who were smiling like crazy men.

"Did you fucking see that? Christ. She caught that—and then— woosh they were all like, 'hot, hot,' wow. Bloody awesome." Zane didn't seem capable of shutting up.

"Zane, did you by chance sell your soul to the devil or a demon?"

He looked taken aback.

"Of course not. I don't like that evil bullshit. It's nasty. And trust me, I've seen the movies. It never works out like the devil promises."

I shook my head. "I'm serious. Back before you became a rock god, did you do something stupid? Make any promises you can't keep?"

He held up both hands. "I swear to you, I've never done anything like that."

"Well, that seals it. I guess we'll be going to London." Damn. I really wanted to go home and feel Sam's arms wrapped around me and sniff that patchouli and sandalwood he always wears. Just the thought of him made me hot.

Zane reached out and hugged me. "Thank you. Thank you for saving my life tonight."

I laughed again. The prime minister noticed our driver was in a bit of shock. I drove us back to the hotel, and we got the man some medical attention. It's not every day that regular folks see a witch go up against a gang of stupid warlocks.

The worst part of today was calling Sam.

"Hey babe, can't wait for you to get home," he said when he picked up the phone. He sounded cheerful for the first time since, damn, I can't remember when.

"Man, I can't wait either. I really need to wrap myself around you."

We both laughed.

I cleared my throat. "But there's been a bit of a hiccup. A small one."

He sighed. "You can't come home for a couple of weeks because Azir needs you to rush off on some grand adventure." I heard the hurt in his voice.

Okay. So it would be one of those kinds of conversations. Stop it. He's tired and still doesn't feel well. Don't make it worse. See, my instinct is to fight back, but I'm trying to learn to stay calm. If I want this to work, and I do, I have to see it from his perspective.

"Actually, Azir's off doing his own thing. It's the PM that needs me to go to London. Um, to help a friend."

"And? Come on Bron, just tell me who the friend is and let's get this over with." Anger tinged his voice.

"Well, you know I can't tell you specifics, but it involves

Zane. There's someone, well really a bunch of idiot warlocks are after him, and I can't just . . . Sam, it's my job to protect people. I can't let them go off and get killed."

There was a long silence.

He cleared his throat and blew out a big breath. "Sorry, I'm being an ass. I just miss you. Really. You do what you have to. I'll try not to be such a jealous butthead and you get home as soon as you can."

I laughed.

The sudden change of attitude was shocking but welcome. "Trust me, I wouldn't be so understanding if the tables were turned. All you need to know is I love you more than anything, and there's no place I'd rather be than in your arms."

"Oh Bron, that was almost romantic." He made silly kissing noises. "By the way, did you have the dream about the sundae? I put down my shields just for you."

I chuckled so hard I couldn't breathe. "You bad, bad boy. And yes I did. You make sure to run to the Piggly Wiggly so that we have both of our houses stocked with plenty of chocolate syrup."

He fake moaned. "Crap Bron, do you know what you're doing to me?"

I was feeling a little breathless myself. "Yeah, well I'm feeling it too, big guy, trust me. Soon. We'll be together soon. Let me go catch the bad boys then we'll spend a whole weekend eating junk food off of one another."

"Sounds like a plan." I heard the smile in his voice. I love Sam's smile, just thinking of it makes my heart go ba-boomp.

So here I sit on a white fur-covered couch waiting for Zane's private jet to take off. There's fur everywhere. Thank goodness it's fake. I'm not some big PETA person, but I don't like the idea that some fox gave his life for a pillow. It seems so sad.

The PM's taking his own jet. I'm not sure how I ended up alone with Zane. Well, there's his assistant, Georgette, but she's got her head stuck in her laptop and it doesn't look like she's coming up any time soon.

It wouldn't be so bad, but he's so damn touchy-feely and he makes me drink champagne. I've had two glasses and we're still on the tarmac. My poor jet is not far from here. I can't wait to get her up in the air and fly home.

But that will be awhile. For now I have to figure out a way to tell Zane to back off, in a nice way. That whole let's-be-friends speech that we all love so much.

Damn, are those Godivas he has in his hands? Bastard.

Five

Saturday, or is it Sunday? 11 P.M. (I'm in time zone hell again. Have no idea what day it is.)
Bournemouth, England
Spells: 4
Charms: 3
Impressed witches: 1

What is it about men and their castles? On the way out of the airport, Zane decided we wouldn't be staying in London. Instead we're heading out to his country home in Bournemouth. It's supposed to be some kind of seaside resort town.

It feels like we rode in the limo for hours, but I think that's because I'm so tired from fending off Zane's advances. Oh, he's never really forward about it. There's a touch on the knee there, a brushing back of the hair here. Geez. The man is too touchy-feely for me.

We drove by the sea, I smelled the freshness of it, but it was too dark to see anything.

Zane's "country house" is a friggin' castle. It sits on the edge of a cliff. Again it was dark, but the outline of the house seemed to go on for miles when we drove up. The inside is the antithesis of his jet, which is over-the-top opulent.

His home is lavish but in a very homey English way. There's lots of chintz, and flower patterns mixed with suits of armor. But it all works in a weird way.

I don't know why people have to name the rooms in their houses, but I'm in the Daisy Suite. I know, I know. The name brings about visions of bright flowered wallpaper. But in truth the only daisies were in a vase on the bedside table. The room is a soft shade of blue and it's monochromatic, except for the crisp white sheets. The bathroom is a bit over the top with blue and white marbled walls and gold fixtures, but hey. There's lots of vanilla bubble bath so it's not all bad.

I tried to call Sam, but my cell phone isn't getting a good connection here. I'll have to try again tomorrow.

For now, I'm going to catch some z's.

Monday, noon

I've been left to my own devices this morning, which of course means I've done nothing but think of Sam. I've been wondering what he's doing today. And I dreamed about him again last night. This time we were up against a wall and I had my legs around his waist. He had my hands above my head. Oh, yeah baby.

I was so disappointed when I woke up and realized he wasn't there.

Zane's working in his studio, located in the east wing of the house. I hung out there for a bit, while he worked with some of his bandmates on a new song. They were busy and I didn't see any way he could get into trouble.

So, I've decided to take a walk on the beach. The weather's warm, and I could use a bit of nature to recharge.

Oh, while I was trying to find my way back to my room from the studio, I snagged a small table to use as a workstation. I've loaded it with the necessities to track down the people behind Zane's troubles. I've also plugged in my laptop to do some searches. I'm going to look at news stories covering his concerts to see if there are any similarities he may have missed.

I had e-mails from my favorite wizard, Garnout. He's going to be out of contact for a few days. He owns a magical store in Manhattan, but it was closed while I was there. He's says he's checking into a situation. That's his code for "something really nasty is coming down the pike and he's gearing up for a war." I sent him a note that if he needs me I'll be there.

But for now, I'm going outside to gather up some good old Mother Nature and hold her close. After a week in Manhattan, I really need some fresh air and trees.

Tuesday, I A.M.
I can't believe how late it is. My body clock is way off the mark. I guess it's okay. Zane keeps rock star hours for the most part. He usually wakes somewhere between 2 and 4 P.M. I've been doing research for the past several hours and just had dinner in my room.

He dined downstairs with the band. Last night they were a rowdy crowd, and though I had fun, I need to get going on Zane's problem.

I've researched some of the articles regarding Zane's concerts and other than the strange sickness, there hasn't been much out of the ordinary. The details of the bodyguard's death were gruesome. The article intimated that drugs were involved, but I don't think it's true. The newspapers here tend to do much more sensational stories than what we have at home. Oh sure, we have some tabloids that do that too, but all of them here seem to be really celebrity-heavy.

And the funniest thing. When I did a search on Zane, two million sites came up. No exaggeration. I clicked on a few and they were shrines to the rock star. Photos, articles, favorite Zane phrases.

But the most interesting and sad thing I found was a story about Zane's brother. The brother and wife were killed in a fiery car crash involving a slick road and a cliff, not too far from this house. Zane had made no comments to the press, but I wondered if there might be some kind of connection.

It only happened a few months ago and I wondered why Zane hadn't said anything. The saddest part is they left a little girl behind, Zoë. I'm curious what happened to her.

Oops, door.

2 A.M.

Spells: 1

That was Zane. He'd spied the light on under the door and decided to see what was up. His room is at the other end of the house, but I didn't bring that up. He acted like he just needed to talk.

"So luv, busy, busy, I see." He made himself comfortable in the squishy chair by the fireplace.

"Kind of. I've been doing some research on you." I pointed to the laptop. "I think your name must be up there in the top two of Internet searches. Right there with porn."

He coughed and laughed at the same time. "Look a little closer, dear, and you may see me in some of those lusty pictures. I had some pretty desperate times in the early days."

"Oh really. Hmmmm. So just how desperate?" I crossed my arms against my chest and waited for an answer. This might be good.

"Well, I had this manager at the time, Roger Harris, who insisted I do every single interview. I was barely eighteen and didn't know better. So when the editor of *Glow* wanted me naked in bed with three women, I did it. Unfortunately, I forgot that there were cameras involved, and the women, well, were quite proficient and things got very wicked, very fast.

"Of course, once I made some money I bought those negatives for a hefty sum, but they still end up on the Internet every once in a while."

I have to admit I fanned my face at the idea of Zane getting it on with three women. I mean who the hell wouldn't?

"So, we can add porn star to your list of credits. Lovely."

We both laughed.

"Well, there are things I've done that I'm not so proud of." He shook his head. "But I never sold my soul to a demon or anyone else, for that matter. I promise. Don't look at me that way."

I must have been frowning, but it wasn't because of what he'd said. I needed to ask him something important. "I wasn't thinking that. It's just well, look . . . there's no easy way to ask this. I read about your brother's death." I paused.

Zane's smile melted off his face. His blue eyes looked haunted.

I wanted to reach out to him, but couldn't. I needed the truth. "It can't be easy to talk about, but I need to know what happened. That's the only way I can decipher if the accident had anything to do with your current troubles."

Zane leaned his elbow on the edge of his chair and put his forehead in his hand. "There's no way the two incidents are related. My brother didn't have anything to do with my career. He's—he was a banker. His wife was in advertising. They were on the way to the house when the car spun out of control. It could have been an animal, or just that the roads were wet. The police say the car made several circles as my brother tried to regain control. They could tell from the marks on the road, but he couldn't get it back."

His voice was quiet, somber. I knew he didn't want to talk about it. I also knew he felt responsible, for some reason.

"Zane, why do you feel so guilty? You had nothing to do with it."

He leaned back and stared at me. "I'd insisted we all meet out here to get away from the paparazzi. In the city I can't take a shit without it being front-page news. They didn't really want to come, but it was my birthday, and . . ."

Crap. His brother died on Zane's birthday. That is major, major suckage.

"Where is their daughter, Zoë? She's mentioned in the article."

He looked up, focusing on the window to my left. "She's at boarding school. She came to live with me for a while. I think she blamed me in some way. She's only eight. I worry about her all the time. I wonder if she'll ever be happy again. I want to know if she's feeling okay."

"I could help you." I don't know why I said it. Maybe because he was so forlorn and I could feel the love he had for his niece. He genuinely cared for the child.

"How?" The shadows eased from his face and he looked hopeful.

"If you have something of hers, I can tap into her mind. I can get an idea of how she's doing. I won't be too intrusive, just kind of a checkup."

He leaned forward. "You can actually see what she's thinking? I thought you felt things, emotions. I had no idea. That's brilliant."

"Yes. But please don't tell the world. Okay? It's not something I broadcast."

A wicked grin spread on his face. "Can you tell what I'm thinking now?"

I snorted. "I don't have to read your mind, you pervert. I can tell by looking at you. Now stop it and find something of Zoë's for me." If I don't know someone well, something tactile helps me find them faster.

He left for a few minutes and came back with a small stuffed monkey. "She sleeps with this when she's here."

Handing it to me, he paused. "Can you really do this?"

"Zane, just give me the damn monkey." I took it from him and closed my eyes. Zoë's elfin face came into my mind. So sweet. A tiny pug nose, long lashes against her cheeks. Sound asleep. I gently nudged her dreams. And I must have gasped because Zane grabbed my arm.

"Bronwyn, stop. What's wrong?" He held on tight. I shook him away.

"Give me a minute." I let the dream play out. She saw her parents happy, talking about a party, but she couldn't go.

"*Please Mummy, I promise to be a good girl.*"

Her mother touched her cheek. "*Zoë, you're always a good girl. It's just that this is a grown-up party and Uncle Zane's house can be a little wild. I know it's hard for you to understand. But you'll be so much happier here with Mr. Tuttles and Nanny Bee.*"

"*No, no Mummy. I want to go. I can be a big girl, I promise.*" Zoë cried out as her parents hugged her good-bye.

"*There's my good poppet.*" Her father smoothed her dark bangs from her face. "*We'll bring you back a special surprise. Perhaps something for you and Mr. Tuttles to play with.*"

Through the large window she watched them pull away. She squeezed Mr. Tuttles, the large stuffed elephant, close. "*Stupid heads. They can just go to their stupid, stupid party. I hope a big monster eats them.*"

Then the tears came and even more so when Uncle Zane came to talk with her. Her mum and dad weren't coming home. They were eaten by a big monster, and it was all her fault.

I opened my eyes and told Zane what I'd seen. "She blames herself for her parents' death. Oh, that poor baby. Sadness and such grief. I haven't ever felt anything like it."

Well that wasn't true. When Sam lay dying in the hospital I experienced those emotions too. He'd died more than once on the day he was attacked, and I took the responsibility of it all onto my shoulders. I'd felt like hell. And it was more than any child should ever have to deal with. I couldn't stop a tear from slipping down my cheek. I jumped up and grabbed a tissue.

"Why did you send her back to boarding school?" The words were more scalding than I meant. "I'm sorry, it's just obvious she's grieving for her parents."

He shrugged. "It was what she wanted. I kept her here for the first month. She wouldn't talk. Nanny Bee could barely get her to eat. A difficult situation all the way around. I wanted to take her on tour with me. I thought that might get her mind off of things, but she kept saying she wanted to go back to school. The counselors I spoke with said it might be best, considering that's where she felt the safest." His voice broke. "She's such a strong little tyke. I had no idea.

"I should go and get her and bring her home. I can't bloody well stand this." He jumped up and paced.

I touched his arm. "Hey, calm down. You've been doing the best you could in a really horrible situation. I don't know a damn thing about raising a child, but I do know that it isn't easy. Everyone who does it seems to screw up somehow, yet most of us turn out fine." I sighed. "Hell, that didn't sound as helpful as I meant. Maybe she could come over for the weekend?"

"Yes, and I'll call Nanny Bee. She'll know all of Zoë's favorite things." He grabbed me and kissed me on the mouth. "Thank you. I know that's not appropriate. But so far this week you've saved my life and have possibly given me a way to get through to my Zoë."

I scrunched up my face. "Okay, but if you kiss me again I'm going to pop you one."

He stopped on his way to the door and turned around. "Oh, that's funny." Then he left.

Jerk. I was serious.

Six

Tuesday, noon
Spells: 13
Wards: 15
Charms: 3

I've set up protection spells and wards everywhere around Zane's property, including his vehicles, and made him a talisman to wear around his neck or put in a pocket. The amber slows when evil is near.

There's just one problem: Until someone actually tries to harm him, I can't tap into the evil that is after him. The warlocks from the other night didn't leave anything behind. If I hadn't been bourboning it up at the club, I might have thought of grabbing at least one of their cloaks.

Doesn't matter. Zane's decided we're going out tonight. The man says he can only stay cooped up for so long. I find it difficult to understand how anyone can be bored with a thirty-room mansion, but then I'm not a grotesquely rich rock star.

So the big plan is to do a little shopping this afternoon in London. Can't say I really mind that, though it is more difficult to protect charges in large cities where so many people are hanging out.

If I were really honest though, another attack would help me ferret out who's behind this crap. So either way, it's win-win. Besides I just happened to notice on the Internet that Harrods is having a huge sale. I hope we can get over there. Zane has upscale boutiques in mind, but we'll see.

I need some basics. I'd only packed for one week in New York, and nothing for the beach. If Zane's bad guys don't show themselves, I may be here a while.

7:30 P.M.

London

We're at Zane's house here in London. It's much more modern than what I expected. Lots of clean lines, dark wood and white furniture.

Except in my room, which is red and yellow. Sounds horrible, but it isn't. Wouldn't have it in my house, but hey, I'm not one of the world's most famous celebrities.

Speaking of which, today was actually fun. We did hit the boutiques. Most of which had clothes that were, well, let's just say not exactly my style. I did find one pair of jeans that make my ass look like a supermodel's. Maybe not *that* great, but better than usual.

I also found a black leather jacket with lots of inside pockets. Those come in handy when I'm trying to carry around a bunch of charms or other magical utensils. Of course, I won't be able to wear it for a few months because it's so hot. But that's okay.

Now Zane, on the other hand, dropped twenty grand at Lithos. On four pairs of leather pants and some boots. The pants are custom fit and all different colors. I never realized how buff he is, but I guess he has to stay in shape to run around and jump like he does onstage.

Then he dropped another fifty thousand at Harrods. He bought clothes, toys for Zoë, jewelry. Oh, my God. I'd never seen anyone spend so much cash so fast, and I've shopped for years with my mother. She's a pro. I don't know many English professors who are obsessed with the latest from Prada and Michael Kors, but my mother is.

But she has nothing, and I mean nothing, on Zane. He's generous to a fault, though. There was a little girl staring at a stuffed bear as big as she was, and he bought it for her. A two thousand dollar toy. Her mother protested until Zane worked that charm of his.

"Lovely woman, the child obviously needs the bear." He took her hand. "Look how it speaks to her." As if on cue the child hugged the humongous toy. I swear the bear smiled. Totally creeped me out.

"Now, that child simply can't be deprived. She needs that toy, and it needs her. And if you let her have it, I'll leave ten tickets for you and your friends at the will call for the concert next month."

The woman gasped and blushed. "Oh, oh. I'm sorry. You don't have to do that. I just didn't want to take advantage of your kindness. I—Well, thank you, Zane. She'll treasure it always."

We walked away, and Georgette made notes in her book to pay for the purchase.

I like Georgette. At first I thought she was a bit of a doormat, but it's quite the opposite. She sort of keeps Zane in line. Well, she lets him spend his money of course, but just when it seems he might slip off into the dark side she pulls him back.

Hard to explain, but I'm glad he has her.

She's kind of cute with her charcoal bobbed hair, eyebrow ring and bright red lipstick. I heard Zane mention she had a beau, but I don't know when she'd see a lover. She's on call twenty-four/seven. Anytime Zane needs something, she's there.

Oh, and the sunglasses. The man bought five thousand dollars' worth of sunglasses. I think it would have been closer to ten thousand, but Georgette whispered something in his ear. He shook his head and told the saleswoman he changed his mind.

Anyway, he wants go to someplace called the Supper Club. He promises food, dancing and lots of fun. We'll see. I noticed something about him today. The more money he spent the happier he became. The day began with him in a foul mood. I wondered if it was from our talk last night, but I didn't ask.

Maybe that's how he buries his pain, by being a shopaholic. We all have our vices. Mine happen to be blowing up people, and binging on Sno Ball cupcakes from Hostess.

What the hell's that buzzing sound?

8 P.M.

Witches who are rolling their eyes: 1

That was Zane making weird noises outside my door. I can't believe that giant goober. He had leather pants made for me to wear tonight, and he wouldn't take no for an answer. He also gave me a cute little black lacy top. It's V-necked and backless. Shows a great deal more skin than usual, but hey. And then there are the shoes. There's no way in hell I can walk in these.

I've worn Christian Louboutin shoes before, thanks to my mother, but these are extraordinary. They're leopard print pumps. And I can't believe I'm doing this, but damn if I'm not going to try and wear them. Now if I can just get these damn pants over my hips.

Zane swore the leather would stretch. We'll see.

3 A.M.

Drunk witches: 1

Okay, I have to stop dancing because that leads to drinking. Which wouldn't be such a bad thing if the drinking were water but it isn't. That horrible Zane totally exploited my love for bourbon. I don't know the name of it, but it's the smoothest shit I've ever had. I mean, whooooo. That first glass went down and all the tension left my body.

We did dine at the club. Nothing too out of the ordinary, although people here really seem to love lamb. I can't get into it.

Ick. Bourbon burp. Just thinking about that poor baby lamb is making me sick. Or maybe it's the six, no eight glasses of that wicked bronze liquid.

So, for dinner I had gazpacho and chicken with giant mushrooms. Maybe they were portabellas, I don't know. It was good. All that crap about English food is just that, crap. It's pretty damn great as far as I'm concerned.

Then we danced. Had to work off all those calories. At first it wasn't so easy with the heels and leather pants. Finally, I just kicked off the shoes and cuffed my pants. I'm sure I looked quite the sophisticate.

Ack, another bourbon burp. Nasty.

I was so tired and we left. Then the cameras. I'm fairly certain I've lost part of my eyesight. Seriously. Blinded by the light. Hey, isn't that a song?

Anyway, we made it back to the red and yellow room. Oh, man. Now it's making me dizzy.

Note to self: Do not look at wallpaper when drunk.

Oooooh. Bathroom.

That was disgusting.

'Nother note to self: Bourbon, bad, bad, bad.

How the hell am I going to get out of these damn pants?

2 P.M.

My head hurts. Have I mentioned that bourbon is the devil's brew? We should bring back prohibition—Hell, I know better than to do this to myself.

I mixed a few greens with a real Coke, and I'm waiting for the herbs to kick in. I hate Zane. I saw him outside getting ready to take a swim in the pool. I'd go out for some sun, but I'm chafed. That's right boys and girls. Falling asleep drunk in your leather pants can lead to skanky skin the next day.

Argh! So embarrassing. Thank God I have one flowy cotton skirt. I'll throw that on with a T-shirt. And see if my eyes can handle the sunlight.

Oh, the good news: I had the most amazing dream. Sam must have opened his mind for me again, and baby I just slipped right in.

We were in my new office at home. I was typing on the computer and he came up from behind and hugged me. The next thing I knew I was bent over on the desk while he was pounding into me from behind. Amazing. And it all felt so real.

I tried to call him to see if he had dreamed the same thing, but he didn't answer.

Think I'll call him again.

5 P.M.

Oh, what a crappy, crappy day. Turns out those photographers weren't just shooting Zane. I was in the big fat middle of every London tabloid this morning. Zane thought it was sooooo amusing.

Please God, if you love me, don't let those pictures make it to the States. Please, please, please. We were also on the UK version of *Entertainment Tonight*, where they pronounced me the new queen to the king of rock and roll. Oh. Horrid, horrid people, the paparazzi. It almost makes me feel sorry for those Hollywood types who complain about their invasion of privacy.

As if I'd date someone like Zane. Oh, he's handsome and charming, but I just don't feel it.

I don't care that much about what people think, but it does feel invasive. I know one thing: I'm not drinking another drop of liquor while I'm here. Not one sip. Nada. No more.

9 P.M.

Okay, so that's disappointing. I tried to call Sam again and he still doesn't answer. I don't care that it's three in the morning there. My friend Kira called and said Sam's really pissed.

She heard from Margie that they were all standing around watching the big screen at the nursing home. The noon news report came on and they flashed the picture of Zane and me coming out of the club.

"When the news anchor said, 'Meet Zane's flavor of the

month,' Sam threw a medical chart across the room and stormed out. No one's seen him since," Kira told me. I could tell she was uncomfortable, but she knew I'd want to know what was going on.

"Kira, you know it's all idiotic. Sam should too. He and I just talked about this." I threw my hands up in frustration. "I mean me and a rock star, come on."

"Well, Bron, actually it's not such a reach. I mean just a few months ago you were hooked up with a sheik. Not technically, but you know what I mean. And Sam, well he hasn't been himself lately. We tried to invite him over to dinner but he said he didn't need to be coddled by your friends. He kind of pissed Caleb off."

Caleb is my brother's best friend and he had met Kira through me. While he was supposed to be looking out for me, he ended up falling in love with the town librarian. He still looked after my place when I was gone, when he wasn't off writing his magazine articles as an investigative reporter.

Kira continued, "But I think Sam's overtired and not himself. Maybe he went back to work too soon."

I'd wondered the same thing many times the last week.

I sat down on the edge of my bed. I'd bought a calling card so I could call direct on Zane's line, since mine keeps cutting out.

"Maybe he did. I don't know. He healed so fast considering everything he went through. God, Kira, I don't know what to do. I want to come home and straighten out this mess, but I can't leave right now. I have a job to do. And to be honest, he's got to start trusting me or this is never going to work."

Kira sighed. "I'm on your side, Bron, really I am. But I saw the news and I've read the articles. I don't care how secure you are; it would be tough to take. They showed you hanging all over

Zane and both of you had huge smiles. It also looked like you were drunk."

"We were drunk. Fuck, fuck, fuck. Sorry, Kira. Sam won't return my calls. This is just total suckage all the way around."

"Give him some time, let him calm down. Any guy would be angry if he saw his woman with another man like that. But Sam's a good guy. He'll come around. And in the meantime, well, I'll keep an eye on him from a distance." She laughed. "I won't let him know he's being coddled. You just hurry up and get those bad guys so you can come home."

We rang off. Even though I promised to never probe Sam's mind, I tried it. He had his shields up so tight, I couldn't even get a fix on his location. I hope he's okay.

I'm going to concentrate on work now, and I'll take every ounce of my frustration out on whoever is after Zane, because these assholes have totally fucked with my life.

Seven

Thursday, 7 A.M.
London
Spells: 2
Witches who may be without a steady boyfriend: 1

Now I'm mad. Sam still won't call me back. Margie told Kira that he showed up at the nursing home to do rounds, but he wouldn't talk to the staff. He was nice to the patients, as always, but didn't say a word to anyone else unless it was to bark orders.

At least I know he's alive.

We have a meeting with the prime minister in two hours. I'm not in the mood. Really, really not in the mood. It's an emergency mini-summit to deal with some rebel problems in Africa. Much of the aid that is supposed to go to the starving and dying children has been cut off by a rebellion.

I know war is commonplace in this world, but why does it always have to hurt the children? Let the grown-ups blow themselves to bits, but leave the innocents out of it.

While it's only a few dignitaries, there's a possibility our bad guys might show up, so I'm included.

It's just as well. Maybe it will get my mind off my own sucky life.

9 P.M.

Spells: 4

Charms: 2

Potions: 2

Pissed-off witches: 1

I friggin' hate demons. Really. They are nasty sons of bitches that should be eradicated from the face of the earth.

When the meetings ended we ran up to a private club just down the block for some lunch. Beef stew. The guys had black and tans, I stuck with bottled water. Nothing major. Zane and the prime minister talked about what they planned to do for the children. And then it was decided the PM would come out to the country house for the weekend.

The shit happened when we walked out the door. Expecting more paparazzi, I was on guard. I was going to cast a spell on any asshole who even tried to take my picture. I still didn't feel so great from the hangover. And let's face it, I'm depressed. So if anyone messed with me, I had several spells ready to go.

But there were no cameras waiting, just a big smelly Arnok demon. Eight foot, yellowish green skin and spitting acid.

"Nasty bugger," Zane said as he stopped short.

The Arnok went for Zane who ducked and stuck out a foot

like a martial arts pro to try and trip the demon. But the demon didn't budge.

"Prime Minister, go back in the pub and call the local spook squad. I'll try to hold him off." I threw a spell to stop the green monster, but it didn't work.

The PM didn't move inside like I asked, but he did pull out his phone and dial someone.

I held out my hands and chanted, trying to bind the demon to the ground where he stood, before he could attack Zane again.

But my magic didn't work. The demon slung out a fist and knocked Zane into the large wooden door. The PM helped Zane up, while I tried to attract the monster's attention.

I threw a fireball at him. But it only made him roar, "No fire!" And he batted it away. The damn thing was protected by dark magic.

"Zane, pull the talisman out of your pocket and hold it up in front of you and the prime minster. This would be easier if you would both go back inside." I motioned to the door.

"Hell no. We aren't leaving you out here alone," Zane yelled. But he did pull out the necklace and wrapped the black cord around his hand a few times. The amber made the demon flinch. And I knew I needed earth magic.

Just one problem. We're in the middle of London and except for the parks, which were blocks away, there's very little that isn't concrete. I noticed a tree a half block down. If I could touch the bark, I could work the spell. I wondered if the idiot might chase me.

"Oh, look, Mr. Demon. The big, bad witch is getting away." I ran past him and taunted him from down the sidewalk. He looked confused. Zane was his target, but demons love anything that runs. I skipped backwards. "Bet I can beat you to the tree." When he took a step toward me I ran for it.

The ground shook from his heavy steps. Damn, he was a big bastard. A woman started to walk out the door of a shop, but took one look at the demon, and hightailed back inside. No one else was around.

I grabbed hold of the tree. It was dying, but there was enough there to do what I needed. "Bless you Mother Earth for your great bounty," I chanted. Then I wrapped a metaphysical chain around the demon. He stopped in his tracks. Couldn't move.

Except that he spat. Yuck. It landed right on my forearm and burned like Hades had come calling. I kept chanting and he kept spitting. That is, until I put some metaphysical duct tape across those nasty lips of his.

The spook squad, a police force that deals with all demons, warlocks, witches and any other magical being who is misbehaving, came around the corner, screeching to a stop. Four men jumped out, dressed in dark blue matching suits. They used a special rope to lasso the demon and placed a black sack over its enormous head.

They loaded it into the back of the truck. After a few questions for us, they took off.

The limo came around and dropped us all off at Zane's to get cleaned up. I couldn't get the burning to stop and pulled out my little black case.

After cleaning the gaping wound with sila soap, I made a combination of chamomile, aloe and blue ziro paste, which cooled the burn, but it was blistered and smelled horrible.

The prime minister wanted to call in a doctor, but few in the medical profession are knowledgeable about demon burns. I do have a talent for healing, but whatever poison had seeped in had drained my powers. After a few more tries I was able to cool the burning. But it continued to blister.

Wrapping the arm from elbow to wrist with gauze, I shimmied out of my tan slacks and white blouse. The blouse went into the trash; between the acid and the burned fabric it was useless.

I needed to rest. I called Zane on the house phone and told him to send someone to check on me if I didn't wake up in a couple of hours. I washed my face free of makeup, and threw on an oversized T-shirt with tiny hearts all over it. Sam gave it to me a few weeks ago. The thought made me cry.

I sobbed into my pillow for a few minutes and then the next thing I knew I heard whispering and it was totally dark.

"Should we wake her up?" That was the prime minister. "I seem to remember that she needs to sleep in order to regain her strength."

"I don't care, I just want to make sure she's alive. Find a mirror we can stick under her nose." Zane sounded so serious.

It made me laugh. My arm felt tight and hot, but other than that, I was fine.

"I'm alive." I raised up in the bed and pulled the blankets around me.

"Thank God," The PM and Zane said together.

"Was there ever any doubt really? She's terribly hard to kill." That was snippy little Miles, the PM's assistant. I hate the bastard, but it was kind of good to hear his voice.

"Hi Fifi, vacation over?" I once threatened to turn Miles into a poodle, and the name's been stuck in my head ever since. I think I like it.

He knew what I was talking about. "She's obviously fine sir, I think we can go now." Miles sniffed.

"In a moment, Miles. Bronwyn, is there anything we can get you?" The PM sounded worried.

"Maybe I could use some tea and some of those sandwiches like we had yesterday, oh and that chocolate cake, the one with the raspberry filling."

Zane laughed. "She's definitely feeling better. She eats like a cow."

"Hey." I wanted to kick his ass, but I just didn't feel quite up to it. My joints were a little achy. Kind of like the flu.

"Sorry luv, it's just that I don't know where you put it. It all seems to be arranged so perfectly."

There was a snort by the door.

"I heard that, Miles. You guys go on, I'm okay. Oh, wait, did they get any info about the demon? It belonged to someone with powerful black magic."

The PM cleared his throat. "Unfortunately, no. When they took the demon back there was a bit of a ruckus and well, he was disposed of in a way that left no remains."

Shit. There goes my evidence. If I had the demon, I might have been able to trace the magic. No demon, no magic. Square one. Great. At this rate I would never make it home.

Friday, II A.M.
Spells: 2
Charms: 3
Sick witches: I

I've been puking for three hours straight and trying to work at the same time. Man, this sucks.

I thought maybe I could use the poison the demon spewed into my arm to trace the magic that had controlled him. No such luck. But now that the spook brigade is involved I have them looking into where the demon may have come from. Usually there's an infestation, and they can track down and eradicate them. If I didn't feel like crap, I'd like to help them.

Once again, back to the beginning with this thing. I have a gang of cloak-wearing wannabe bad guys. An Arnok demon, and the death of Zane's brother. The events are too close not to be related.

And I've been thinking about that voice. Maybe it's my muddled mind, but when the warlock in New York spoke he sounded just like that evil Blackstock. I remember that tone reverberating in my head when he tried to kill me in my conservatory. I'm crazy. I sent that asshole to hell. There's no way he'd be back.

God, my head hurts. Maybe it's not the demon acid. I could have picked up a summer flu or something. My arm actually looks better, but I feel one hundred times worse.

I'm expected downstairs in a few minutes and have to pretend all is well. If Zane even suspected that I was under the weather he'd have every doctor in town here and probably buy me a Bentley. Since I've saved his life twice in the last few weeks, he swears he's indebted for life.

Whatever. I just want to find out who the hell is trying to kill him so I can go home.

Eight

Okay, it sounds dramatic but I feel like I'm going to die. I've been taking herbals for the last few days, and it's kept my fever down. But whatever this is it's not good. I'm sick.

On to more important matters. I met Zoë. I'm not much into kids, but she's a cute one. Very polite, and quiet. The thing that gets me is the sadness that emanates from her. She has huge gray eyes that just look right through you, and she drags that elephant I saw in the dream around with her everywhere she goes.

I also discovered she has a touch of magic in her. A witch doesn't really come into her powers until late teens, but I could feel it in her.

I asked Zane if he knew if her mother had been a witch.

He looked at me funny and then ran a hand through his blond curls. "No, no. But it wouldn't matter. She wasn't Zoë's birth mother. My niece is adopted."

Hmmm. Interesting.

"And these problems you've had began when her parents were killed?"

We were standing in his kitchen at the country house, which is as big as a ballroom. Three sinks. Who the hell needs three sinks? And two fridges. Please.

"Bronwyn, what are you getting at? Zoë has nothing to do with these attacks. My God, she's a child."

"Calm down, rock star. I didn't say she did. It's just that nothing is ever really coincidence. What's happening to you is a puzzle I have to put together, and I've got to look at all aspects of the situation."

"I thought the whole point of bringing you here was so you could just sort of wave your hand and make it all go away," he mumbled.

Man, yesterday I was the big hero. Oh, how fast the glory fades.

"Trust me, if I could wave my hand, and get rid of the trouble, I would. As you've seen, it doesn't work that way. I don't have a single person I can tap into."

At that point I bent over in pain and then ran for the sink. I guess I don't have to say how embarrassing it is to lose your breakfast in front of a client. A client who happens to be one of the most famous celebrities in the world.

"What the bloody hell? Why didn't you tell me you're ill? Matt," he yelled. "Get in here. Our girl's sick."

Who is Matt?

When the prime minister came in I almost fell over. Great. It never occurred to me he had a first name. If I hadn't been about to pass out, I would have laughed.

"Matt, what do we do?"

The prime minister pulled out his phone. "Don't worry Brother, I know what to do."

Brother? As the lights dimmed before my eyes, I whispered, "Call Garnout."

I woke up this morning in Garnout's guest room in his Manhattan apartment. I have no idea how I got here, but my mother was sitting beside my bed.

"Oh, honey, how do you feel?" she asked when I opened my eyes. There wasn't a hair out of place on her head. She always looks so immaculate. My mom is as close to perfect as they come. Since witches age slower than most, people always think we're sisters because she looks so young.

I blinked twice and moved all my body parts. "Better." My voice was a harsh whisper.

My arm had healed completely. But the worried expression on my mother's face told me things had been rough going.

"What happened?"

"Well, it seems the demon's acid made its way to your heart. When you whispered Garnout's name he heard you. Neither of us is sure how. Before the prime minister could call him, he was there in the kitchen. He flashed you back here, and I'm certain he kept you from dying." Her voice caught.

I tried to sit up, but my head was still dizzy. Mom stood and plumped the pillows behind me.

She dabbed her nose with a tissue. "He called not long after he brought you here." Her eyes welled with tears. "Oh, baby, I've just never been so frightened. We almost lost you twice."

I squeezed the hand she put in mine and brought it to my cheek. "Sorry. I'd tried to get the poison out of my system. I invoked every healing spell and potion I could find, but nothing seemed to work. By the time I realized how sick I really was, well, I guess it was too late."

"Don't worry about it now, dear. Garnout knew exactly what to do." She pushed my hair away from my face.

"Where is he?"

"When your vital signs stabilized I sent him to the shop and your dad back to the hospital. They were both driving me crazy. Hovering and clucking, like mother hens. Your dad wanted to try antibiotics, and Garnout poured one potion after another down your throat. I'll call them in a minute to let them know you're awake."

We talked for a few more minutes and she gave me my journal to write in. She knows how important it is for me to get everything on paper. I'm kind of paranoid that someday a warlock will get the best of me, and no one will know what happened.

Oh, man I'm tired. Think I'll rest for a bit.

Thursday, 2 P.M.
Bored witches: 1

They finally let me out of bed today. Since I woke up, my mom, dad and Garnout have been waiting on me hand and foot. It's quite disconcerting. We've played cards, listened to music and I've read the latest *Witch's Journals* until my eyes are crossed.

I even had "the talk" with my mother. No, not the birds and the bees. The why-does-my-boyfriend-hate-me talk.

"That man loves you." My mother smiled as she laid down her sixth hand. She's a killer gin player and has no sympathy for a sick daughter. "I know he does."

I almost threw my cards at her. "Let's play Texas Hold 'Em." At least then I might have a chance of winning. "And he may have loved me once, Mom, but I almost died and he hasn't even called."

"I told you, we haven't been able to get in touch with him, and Kira says he's out of town."

Kira had told me the same thing. She and Caleb have been so worried about me. I'm lucky to have friends like them.

"So what should I do? How do I get him to love me again?" The words sounded desperate, even to me.

"Baby, you can't make someone love you. I saw those pictures of you and that Zane fellow. Sam's a great guy, but we all have our pride. It couldn't have been easy for him to see."

I understood that. Really, I did. "But why can't we at least discuss it like adults? He won't even answer my calls."

Mom shuffled the cards. "Oh, honey, give him time." She held up a hand. "I know that isn't what you want to hear, but men have to mull things over a bit. Trust me, your father and I have had our differences. There's been lots of mulling on both our parts."

I'd never heard my parents argue much. Once in a while when Dad got tired of going to charity events, or when Mom had to teach late at night and he worried about her safety.

She was a pretty powerful witch, though she turned away from the craft. My dad didn't need to worry about her. We played for a little longer. I won one hand out of five, and she'd never played the game before. Did I mention my mother's perfect?

This afternoon, I'm outside in the tiny courtyard below Garnout's apartment. He shares the green space with two other tenants. It's beautiful, and though it's August in New York and about two hundred degrees, the flowers are in full bloom. The jasmine and roses make me think of my own garden back home.

The wizard knows how much I need nature to heal. That's where the majority of my magic comes from and I have to be close to it on a consistent basis to feel good.

His apartment is always tidy, though it's filled with oddities from around the world. I like things a little less pristine, and nature is always messy.

The prime minister, Zane, and several of my friends besides Kira and Caleb in Sweet have called to check on me. I learned that Zane and the PM are stepbrothers. I don't know why one of them didn't think it important to mention the fact they were related. That opens up a whole new set of possibilities as to why someone is trying to hurt Zane.

Garnout's brought in Callie Lane to help. She's a witch who's based in Sydney, Australia. I've met her at a couple of the conferences and she's one of the few witches that could give me a run for my money. Luckily, we get along fairly well. She's kind of tough but I know she'll protect the prime minister and Zane with her life.

Normally I'd feel horrible about someone taking on my charges, but Garnout says it could be a few weeks before I'm back to normal.

"Bronwyn, remember when you were attacked by Blackstock?" Garnout began the lecture, as he paced in front of my bed.

"It's not like I can forget one of the worst days of my life." I rolled my eyes and he smirked.

"Well this attack had ten times the black magic behind it that Blackstock's did."

That got my attention. "What?"

"It made its way to your heart, and it was quite purposeful, as if it were specifically made for your body chemistry. I've got a lab studying it, and even they are stymied." He pulled on his long beard.

"What are you talking about? It was just a stupid acid-spitting demon."

"The instrument was the demon, but the poison he spat at you was made with a dark magic. Something we haven't seen for years."

"But the demon was after Zane. I just happened to get in the way."

Garnout sighed. "Dear, you know there is no such thing as a coincidence. The scenario was carefully orchestrated. They made it seem like Zane was the target, but the poison wouldn't have worked the same way in his body. He would have felt bad for a day or two, and then been fine. No, someone wanted you out of the way."

He sat down on the edge of the bed. "I've done some checking and you'll be happy to know there aren't any mystical hits out on you at present. It may be the first time in five years that's happened."

I laughed. I did seem to be a great big target for bad guys. That's why I moved away from New York. Every time I took a walk, or tried to eat at a restaurant some stupid warlock would cause trouble. I moved to Sweet, Texas, to avoid all that. The town had its share of magical folks, but so far none of them wanted to kill me.

Maybe with the exception of my recently ex-boyfriend, who wouldn't talk to me. I'm mad because he hasn't called, and sad because I love him so much it hurts. If I could just see him, I know we could sort this out.

"Well, I'll delve a little deeper and see what I can find. We are trying to trace the magic, but so far we haven't found much, except it originated in Europe somewhere. Do you know of anyone who would wish you harm?"

Normally, yes. But to be honest I hadn't pissed anyone off in at least a few months. Well, that I could remember, anyway.

I told him no, but he didn't look like he believed me.

"How are your talks going with those corporate covens that moved into town?" I asked, trying to change the subject.

He frowned and shook his head. "Bad business, pardon the pun. Magic and money seldom mix. I don't know what those witches and warlocks are thinking." He stood. "I know there's something dark involved with them, but I haven't found proof."

I smiled. The Wizard Garnout thrived at keeping the world's magical balance intact. It's what kept him hanging around in this dimension for so many years.

"Is there anything I can do to help?"

He reached down and patted the top of my head. "Just heal." He sent a healing spell into my body and I instantly relaxed. "If you behave, I may let you go home over the weekend. Why don't you call your friend Caleb and see if he can come get you? I don't think you need to be on a commercial flight with your immune system so compromised."

"Oh, I'll be fine by then. I can fly myself home, my jet's still at the hangar." I couldn't wait to get back up in the air.

"No, Bronwyn, you aren't fine. This thing attacked your heart. Think of it as a heart attack. Your body needs more time to heal. You are a witch and that helps speed the process but you can't push these things. Call your friend, or the deal's off, and you'll be stuck with me for another few weeks."

Argh! I'd just convinced my mom and dad that I didn't need to go to their house to recoup. I sure didn't want to be stuck here. So I called Caleb. He needed to come to Manhattan anyway. He's working on a freelance piece for the *Times*.

I can't wait to go home. And I'm especially curious to find out why Sam, who was my boyfriend up until a few days ago, hasn't even bothered to call. Kira said he was out of town, and may not have heard about it. But still.

I wanted to call him and leave a message. "Hey, I almost died. Thought you'd like to know." But thought better of it.

When I get home I'm determined to at least talk to him. I want him to know what a jerk he's been.

Nine

Spells: 0

Boyfriends: 0

Skinny witches: I (*I've lost twelve pounds, almost had to die to do it, but hey*)

Damn, I'm glad to be home.

I've said it a million times but as soon as my feet hit the ground in Sweet, I feel better. On the way to the house from the hangar, we stopped at Lulu's to pick up some takeout. Ms. Johnnie and Ms. Helen, who own the café, hugged me so hard I couldn't breathe.

"Girl, Kira told us how sick you've been and we've just been prayin' and prayin'." Ms. Helen held my hand. She was dressed in lime green Capris and a T-shirt that said Come on and Get It.

"We even fixed you two kinds of pie, chocolate and raspberry, and Helen's got a box of fried chicken and mashed potatoes ready for you. Oh, and we threw in some green beans with bacon. A girl can't have too much fiber."

I smiled. The bacon fat in those green beans far outweighed any health benefits from the vegetable.

"Oh, I missed you two." I patted both of their arms. Ms. Johnnie had on a red outfit that looked vaguely like hot pants from the 1960s. A thick white belt, and white cowboy boots finished off the outfit. The scary thing is that she's almost seventy, and they didn't look that bad.

Both of them were trying a new hair color. I think it might have been red, but under the lights in the café it looked purple.

The smell of the fried chicken made my stomach grumble. It'd been more than a week since I had a decent meal. The New York contingent were of the starve a fever variety. All I'd had to eat was broth, bread and herbal teas Garnout made. Of course I'd lost a lot of weight, so it wasn't so bad.

Caleb picked up the bags of food and kissed both women on the cheek. "Thank you for taking care of the food tonight. Kira and I appreciate it."

"Oh you handsome boy, you know we'd do anything for our girl Bronwyn," Ms. Helen chided.

She turned to me. "Now you get on home and curl up with some of those fashion magazines. Nothing like staring at sexy shoes from them designers. Just the other day Johnnie and I ordered some of those delicious Jimmy Choos right off of eBay. Can't wait for them to get here."

You know that's why I love this place. The idea of those two old broads running around in last year's Jimmy Choos made me smile the rest of the day.

I still haven't heard from Sam. Word is he's at some medical conference in Utah. Whatever. I can't believe he hasn't even tried to call me. He has to know what happened in London.

Part of me wants to fight for him and make him understand that what he saw on television and in the papers wasn't true. Then there's another part that's disappointed he didn't trust me.

I'm home now, curled up on the couch watching television. Thank God for TiVo. I'm catching up on all of my favorite shows. I have chicken and pie. A girl really doesn't need much more.

Men are so stupid.

Sunday, noon

The world is a crazy place. Okay, everyone knows that but I swear mine is tilted just a bit to the left.

Kira stopped by this morning. She made tea, brought pastries. Man, I love chocolate-filled croissants.

We talked about everything that happened in Sweet over the last few weeks. It wasn't much. Sweet's a small town.

"Let's see. Well, Ms. Johnnie checked out *The Joy of Sex* for the thirty-sixth time," laughed Kira. "I want to buy her a copy and just leave it at the diner but I don't want to embarass her."

I snorted. "I don't know what that book is going to teach her. Between the men she and Ms. Helen have either dated or married she's got to know all there is."

Kira laughed so hard her tea came through her nose. "No joke. Ouch, that hurt," she said wiping her nose with a tissue.

"Billy Carlton's been trying to get Margie to go out with him. He asked her out in the produce section of the Piggly Wiggly. She's been sweet on him forever, but she told him no. Then he asked her out after church last Sunday. She said she'd think about it.

"She's trying to play hard to get, and it must be working. Friday he showed up at the nursing home with three dozen roses. She finally said yes. They're coming to the party tomorrow night."

"What party?" I put down my croissant. "You're having a party without me?"

"Of course not. It's kind of a party for you. Just a few people. All you have to do is show up. You sit on the couch and let us all adore you and then we make an early night of it. It is a weeknight.

"Everyone misses you and I thought we could do enchiladas, beans and rice if you are up to it. I got instructions from your mom that there is no drinking allowed for a few weeks, so—"

I sat up on the couch. "My mom called you?"

"No, I called her every day to check on you and to make sure you had everything you needed when you came back to Sweet. Sometimes at first, we called a couple of times a day. We were all really worried about you." Her eyes became shiny.

I reached out and touched her arm.

"Kira, I'm okay."

She waved her hand in front of her face to stop from crying. "I know, I'm being silly, but we were so worried about you, Bron. Caleb and I both wanted to come to New York, but your mom told us to stay put. That first night it was all I could do to just sit by the phone and wait for your parents to call." A tiny sob snuck out.

Her sincerity brought tears to my eyes.

"You guys—"

She got up and hugged me. "We love you so much, and we just couldn't imagine this place without you."

It must have been because I've been so sick, but I broke down.

I couldn't stop crying. Everything came out. My anger with Sam, the demons and just the emotion of realizing I'm not indestructible. I forget sometimes.

She cried too for a few minutes, and then we suddenly stopped and giggled.

"Hmmm, well." I tried to catch my breath. "Let's hope that's the end of that."

"Hey, crying is good for you. Or so I've read. It gets some kind of healing endorphins going. So you obviously needed it." She smiled. "Hell, so did I. I've been tied up in knots since you left."

I crossed my legs underneath me and grabbed my tea. The chamomile filled my senses.

"Bron, I've wanted to tell you something for some time, but I can't. I haven't been able to tell anyone. It's so weird." She crossed her arms in front of her chest.

Her tone worried me. She was upset. "What? You know you can tell me anything, Kira. Whatever it is, I'll help you."

She closed her eyes and took a deep breath. When she opened them again she stared right at me.

"I see dead people." She said it so deadpan I couldn't tell if she was joking.

I smiled.

"No, I mean I see dead people for real, Bron. It began when I took over at the library. I'd feel things in that old building. A cold rush of air in certain spots. Something touching the back of my neck." She shivered.

"I thought at first it was just a drafty old place. Then I saw a wisp of something out of the corner of my eye one afternoon.

When I turned to look it disappeared. It happened so fast, I wrote it off."

I wanted to interrupt her. I'd known for months that she might be sensitive to the spirit world. Though she hadn't said anything, I'd noticed she felt something in my house during a girl's night in. In fact, there are always ghosts hanging out where I live. They don't bother me and I don't mess with them.

But like I said, she had to tell me in her own way.

She stood up and walked over to the fireplace. She put her hand against the rough Texas limestone. "Now I see them everywhere, Bron, as well as I see you right now. I think I'm losing my mind."

"Kira, don't be silly. You've probably been sensitive for a long time but have unconsciously blocked it. Do you ever remember being frightened as a child by people you couldn't explain?"

She paced back and forth in front of the coffee table. "I grew up in a house of strange people." Her mom and dad are hippies. Kira tried to leave that life behind as a high-powered corporate lawyer before she came home to take over the library.

"But I do remember having so many imaginary friends that even my parents looked at me funny. You know how they are; you have to be pretty whacked to even get on their radar."

Couldn't keep from laughing. I reached a hand out to her. "Come sit down. It's okay. You can learn to control this, I promise. I'll help you any way I can."

"I've been researching." She rolled her eyes. "I'm a librarian; it's what we do. There are lots of psychics who say they can talk to the dead. Of course, until a few months ago I thought they were insane too." She finally sat back down. "I'm not crazy am I?"

She asked so earnestly, I felt sorry for her.

"Of course not. Well, you're dating Caleb, but other than that I find you perfectly sane."

That made her smile. Caleb has sort of set himself up as my surrogate bro, while mine is in Africa saving the poor and downtrodden. I pretend very hard that I despise him as much as I do my real brother, but I don't.

She sighed. "I can't tell Caleb. I don't think he'd like the fact that his girlfriend is some kind of freak."

"Now you're being crazy. My God, Kira, that man loves you beyond—beyond. So you're a little psychic. Could be worse. You could be a witch." I smiled and squeezed her hand.

"Don't make fun. You're so powerful and wonderful. But I don't want to tell him. I keep hoping that maybe it will go away." She frowned when I started to say something. "I know, but for now let me hope."

There was no way I'd tell her she would only grow more powerful.

"So, if you need me I'm here. I can help you learn to control it. Even how to send the dead people on their way if they get too obtrusive."

"Really? Oh that's good news. I don't mind so much except when they follow me into the bathroom. I couldn't pee the other night because they were all staring at me."

We both giggled.

"So, what about this party tomorrow night?" I stretched my arms over my head. I didn't feel as achy as I did last week, but my muscles were still tight.

"Do you feel like you're up to it? It's just Margie and her

new guy, Billy, Caleb, me and—" She looked down at her fingers.

"And who?"

"Sorry, lost my train of thought. That's it. I thought maybe we could do it at my house, but you still look pale. Would you rather have it here? You don't have to do anything, I'll take care of the house, the food," she smiled, "and of course the decorations."

I didn't really want to leave home, but it would be good to be with the gang again. Sans Sam of course. Stupid, stinky jerk.

I must have frowned.

"Bron, seriously, we don't have to do anything." Kira interrupted my musings.

"No, it's fine. I'm looking forward to it, but let's do it here. I don't think I'm up to going much of anywhere right now."

"No worries." She laughed. "I stole that from you. I'll come by in the morning to get things ready. Oh hey, I was going to put a load of clothes in the wash for you but couldn't find your laundry basket."

"Don't worry about it, Mom did all my laundry before I left. The only thing I'm concerned about is Casper. I haven't seen her since I got back."

My cat doesn't particularly care for me, and the feeling is mutual—still, I worry.

"Oh, I'm sure Casper's fine. She was here day before yesterday. Caleb fixed the pet door."

She picked up the dishes and made sure I had something easy to eat for lunch.

I think it's time for a *Mary Poppins* break. When I'm feeling icky about life, I just pop in the DVD and Julie Andrews sings about spoons full of sugar, and life doesn't seem so bad.

I know, I know. Big bad witch watching *Mary Poppins*. Fuck it, it makes me feel good.

Monday, II A.M.

I worked out in the garden for about a half an hour. It's so hot, even with the coolers in the conservatory. My roses were in sad neglect and all the herbs needed an extra dose of water. Caleb's putting a timer on the new misters so when I'm gone I don't have to worry about getting someone to come over and water them.

I finally gave in and called Sam at home. Then I called his cell. Tried to sound cheery. "Hi Sam, just got back into town. Almost died in London. Thought you'd like to know. And I know it's stupid, but I miss you."

It wouldn't be so bad, but I left the same lame message twice. Desperate. I know.

I've got to get him out of my head. I wish I didn't love him so much.

On the plus side, Kira has cleaned my house and it looks better than it has in weeks. I keep things neat, but she was a wild woman. She even dusted the top of the books, and scrubbed the tubs in all three bathrooms. I don't know why, no one is going to take a bath except me. Anyway, the house smells great. She set candles everywhere and even put our favorite party twinkle lights up.

She came early and did it all before she had to go in to the library. So when I came downstairs, it was to a very clean house. She's a great friend.

Caleb left an avocado sandwich from Lulu's and some chocolate pie in the fridge for my lunch. So it's lunch, a shower, a nap and then the dinner party. It almost feels like life is back to normal.

Well, with the exception that my former boyfriend hates me.

5 P.M.

Wow. I cannot wake up. Gonna run and take another quick shower. I can't decide what to wear. I think I'm leaning toward the halter top Zane bought, and those jeans I love. Maybe if I dress like I feel great, and pretend like I'm better, I will be.

If I ever see another one of those demons I'm going to blow it to hell and back.

Checked with Callie. Nothing unusual is going on with Zane. He and the band are gearing up for a concert tour that's going to start in the United States and then move back to Europe. He'd been doing some club dates to try out new songs, and now they're busy putting the show together.

She sounded bored. There's been a lot of activity with the warlock population in Australia, so she's probably missing her daily duels with the bad guys.

It made me laugh when she asked about Miles.

"What's with that ornery little twit who follows the prime minister around everywhere he goes?" She has a slight accent, but I doubt most people would guess she's from Nigeria.

"That's his assistant, Miles, he comes with the territory. And he's a bothersome ass. Just tell him you'll turn him into a poodle if he gives you any trouble, and he'll leave you alone."

She gave a hearty laugh. "Oh, I could see that ninny with some pink bows over his ears."

I'd had the same thought many days.

We hung up and that's when I took my nap. It was dreamless

for once. Thank goodness. I keep seeing the strangest things in my dreams. Orange eyes that float around, and weird slimy eggs. And I wake up feeling sick.

Darn, it's getting late. Better get that shower and then dress before company gets here.

Ten

*W*ell, the party was a success. Kira outdid herself with the food. We had cheese enchiladas, rice, beans and sopaipillas with honey and butter.

Yummers.

Margie brought Billy, who is a sweet guy and looks like a sandy-haired surfer. But he's all cowboy. Right down to the "Yes ma'am" and "I reckon." A real Southern gentleman, who can tell a joke like nobody's business. He fit right into our little group.

Janet and Mike were also here. She's in the local coven, and helped to drag me in the house after I'd been attacked by Black-stock. I didn't know her at the time, but once I healed, we became good friends. She's one of the few natural witches here in Sweet. She doesn't have a lot of power, but she's got enough to help with healing.

She and her husband are opening a bookstore in town. They've been setting up for the past few months, and have promised to have a healthy dose of magical reference books available. Between Kira's stash at the library and the new store, I'll be covered.

An hour after everyone arrived, my shoulders dropped. Kira and the other women loved my outfit. I left off the leopard print shoes. Four-inch heels seem a little much for a party at home. So the feet were bare, except for the fuck-me red nail polish.

We listened to music and talked about everything. It was so much fun. Just as things were winding down about nine thirty, there was a knock on the door. I was in the kitchen and asked Caleb to get it.

Then there was yelling. "What the hell's going on? Is she okay?" Sam's voice boomed in the other room.

I peeked around the corner and he saw my face.

My stomach hit my toes, and my throat went dry.

"You told me you almost died," he screamed.

God, he was beautiful when he was angry. His skin flushed, his blue eyes glaring. I wanted to punch him for hurting my feelings and kiss him at the same time.

"Hey, she did, buddy, and you need to calm down." Caleb put a hand on Sam's shoulder.

Sam shook him off. "I thought she was on her deathbed, and she's having a damn party."

Caleb started to speak, and I waved him down.

"I was sick, I'm better now. Garnout saved me. I'm sorry I left the message."

He stood and stared at me. His chest was heaving with a lack of oxygen.

"I thought you were dying. I've been out of town and my battery died on the cell. When I checked the messages at home, there were three from your mother, a couple from Kira and then yours." His eyes turned indigo.

"You almost died?" He seemed to have trouble with the idea.

"Yes, wasn't the first time, probably won't be the last." I shrugged and bit my lip to keep from smiling. He wouldn't be this angry if he didn't love me.

He scowled and shook his head.

Kira cleared her throat. "Well, Bron, you need your rest. Kitchen's cleaned up. I'll stop by and get the rest tomorrow. Come on gang, let's go."

She ushered everyone, except Sam, to the door.

Caleb whispered something in her ear. I saw her mouth, "She'll be fine."

Everyone said good-bye. I waved and smiled.

When the door shut, I focused on Sam.

"I'm sorry I left the message like I did. I just—"

He took a step closer to me. "What happened?"

"We were in London when a demon attacked, I fought him off and bound him, but not before he spat acid and screwed up my arm."

Sam looked down at my arm. Then at my chest. I suddenly realized the halter top was an inspired choice.

"I didn't know how powerful the poison was, or that it had

black magic behind it. By the time I realized what happened, it was almost too late. If Garnout hadn't come in time . . . You didn't call me." The hurt of the past few weeks welled in my heart.

I moved past Sam. I don't know if it was the excitement of seeing him or just from the party, but I was suddenly beyond tired. I had a choice of fainting or sitting. I chose the latter.

He rushed to my side. And grabbed my wrist. Not in a sexy way, but in an I'm Dr. Sam way. "Damn, you've overdone it. You're paler than I've ever seen you and your pulse . . . Geez, when in the hell are you going to learn to take care of yourself?"

I was too tired to argue. "Could you yell at me tomorrow? I'm wiped out."

He pulled me up with one hand. "Come on, let's get you upstairs." That's when I noticed something was missing.

"Where's your cane?"

He looked down at his hand. "I don't need it anymore. Stop stalling. I can't carry you up those stairs quite yet, and you look like you're about to crater in less than a minute."

He had a point. My body felt drained of all energy. With his hand on my butt, he half pushed me up the stairs. I made it to the bed and sat down. For the fortieth time since I came home I wondered why I had made one of the guest bedrooms upstairs mine. It would be so much easier to use the master downstairs. There was just something about this room, maybe the view that looked out over the vast plains. I don't know.

Sam went to the dresser and grabbed an oversized Mickey Mouse T-shirt. He undid the halter and then pulled the big shirt over my head. Not even taking time to admire my tits, which he usually does with great abandon. He was in doctor mode and refused to be distracted.

He pushed me back and peeled the jeans off of me. I kind of hoped he noticed how good my butt looked when he followed me up the stairs.

The tiredness overtook me. "Sam?"

"I know Bron, move up and I'll pull the covers over you." His voice was soft and caring.

"Thank you." I snuggled into the covers.

He turned off the light and flipped the ceiling fan on. Even with the air-conditioning, it gets warm in the house. I heard him moving around for a minute. Then he climbed under the covers with me. He pulled my back to him, spooning, and that's the last thing I remember.

When I woke up this morning there was a glass of orange juice on the bedside table, and a note.

"I'll bring lunch. Rest. We'll talk later. Love—S"

So, I'm thinking "Love—S" is a good sign. Even if he's consciously mad at me, his unconscious still loves me. I know it's twisted. I don't care.

We definitely have to get all of this straightened out. He should know by now that I don't have intimate relationships with my clients. Okay, well there was that slight slip with Azir, but that's the only time. I don't kiss clients and I certainly don't sleep with them. And if nothing else happens this afternoon, Sam will know that.

Now I have to find something to wear that will make him think twice. I wish it weren't so warm. Those leather pants look awesome. Oh, I know, the denim shorts. He loves these raggedy shorts I wear to work in the garden. My butt hangs out of the bottom, but I think that's part of the appeal.

3 P.M.

Thoroughly kissed witches: 1

Talk about your afternoon delight. Yum. Sam brought chicken-fried steak, mashed potatoes and blueberry pie from Lulu's. I'm so full all I want to do is take a nap.

Full and happy.

I had found one of his old button-down shirts and tied it around my waist, and put on the skanky shorts. I wanted all guns firing.

He didn't bother knocking, just came into the kitchen where I was mixing some herbal iced tea. His eyes went straight to my ass.

And I smiled.

"So what's in the bag?" I pointed.

As he opened it, the smell of home cooking poured into my kitchen.

He set it on the counter. "The girls sent chicken-fried steak and the fixings. Ms. Johnnie sends her love and an order that you are to clean your plate. You're still a bit on the peaky side, she says."

"The peaky side?" I laughed.

"It's a direct quote."

We didn't talk while he put out the food, and I set the table in the kitchen. I love my kitchen; we recently stained the cabinets and it has umber walls. Very Mediterranean. It's also calming.

Placing the food on the plates, he piled mine high with Southern delicacies.

We both reached for the sugar at the same time, and our fingers brushed. That frisson of energy I feel when he touches me sizzled. I backed off. He took the spoon from the china bowl and added three teaspoons to my glass and then put some in his own.

I looked down at my plate and tried not to smile. It's those intimate gestures that get me. The little things like putting sugar in my glass first.

He pointed to the back of the kitchen where the door led to the conservatory. "How are your plants doing in this heat?"

I guess we had to start somewhere. "Not too bad. They got a little dehydrated when I was gone, even with daily watering. Caleb's set the misters so they come on twice a day now. I can't wait for fall so I can plant some more herbs."

There's also Sam's smell. It's a mix of patchouli and sandalwood. I love it. For me it's like smelling home, which is strange because most of the time my house smells like a mix of vanilla and cinnamon. I'd been so angry with him in London for not believing in me, now all I wanted was to lay my head on his shoulder and sniff him.

I sighed, and he must have mistaken it for sadness.

"Bron, I should probably say I'm sorry about not calling you back." He put his fork down and leaned back in his chair.

I swear I wasn't playing hard to get, but I didn't know what to say. He *should* apologize. So I kept my mouth shut.

"It's not an excuse, but I haven't been myself lately. I still get tired and I'm not sleeping well. Then I saw that newscast, and everyone was staring at me. I could see it in their eyes. 'Poor Dr. Sam,' lost his girl to the big famous rock star."

"Sam . . ."

He shook his head. "And it hurt, Bron. I know now, that nothing happened. But you were all over him and he had his arms around you. It hurt."

Now it was my turn.

"I'm sorry too. I had too much to drink, and the crowd was

pushy. We were more leaning on each other than anything. I saw the pictures, I know what you thought. But that hurts too, Sam. You know how much I love you and that it's not easy for me to love the way we do. And you were ready to toss it all away because of some stupid photographers, who I really need to hex as soon as I can perform magic again."

Garnout said I had to wait at least one more week before I tried anything of the magical persuasion. It didn't matter. My body wasn't cooperating and I doubted I could incinerate a fly at this point.

"I love you too." He said the words but he still had anger in his eyes. "I—" Shaking his head he picked up his fork and dug into his chicken-fried steak.

"Tell me, Sam. What is it?" I wanted to touch him, but we had to get this clear first.

Blowing out a breath, he stared at me. "I'm more angry that you almost died. As angry as I was about the rock star, it paled in comparison to how I felt when I got home and found out you almost didn't make it. I'm not sure I can ever get used to this job of yours. Every time you leave town I'm going to wonder if this is it. Am I going to see you again?"

This is one of the main reasons high witches like me don't do well with boyfriends. The powerful ones, and I'm one of them, usually work as metaphysical bodyguards or hunters. Both jobs are equally dangerous. The bodyguards protect world leaders and other dignitaries; the hunters go after the evil in the world and eradicate it. I do a little of both, which means double the fun.

"I don't know what to say to make you feel better, Sam. I'm not going to quit my job. It's what I am. I thought you could handle that. I want you to handle that. I need you in my life." A tear fell down my cheek. I didn't even know I was about to cry. Just knew I couldn't live without this man. Well, I'd live, but I didn't want to.

He sighed. "I think I need a little time." Holding up a hand, he stopped my rebuttal. "Not like that, I mean to get used to this. I want us to be together too. And I promise to try and not be jealous, but that's going to take some work."

"I have an idea. How about if I try to stay sober on assignments and not get killed? And you worship and adore me at all times."

He laughed hard at that. The tension in the room melted away. Grabbing my arm, he pulled me across to his lap and kissed me. Not in a gentle way, but in an I'm-never-going-to-let-you-go way. I relaxed in his arms and let my body meld into his. He felt so strong and hard. And he tasted like steak and tea. And Sam.

My hands roamed across his shoulders and down his chest. I wanted to undo the buttons on his shirt, but he pushed my hands away.

"None of that," he whispered against my lips.

I pulled away and gave him my evil stare. "And why the hell not? It's been weeks. Hello? What about the worshipping me thing?"

He smiled. "Bron, I talked to Garnout this morning. No sex, no magic, nothing but rest and relaxation for at least another week.

"No," I whined. "It's not fair." I stomped my foot on the floor.

He picked me up and put me back in my chair.

"Now, be a good girl and eat all of your lunch." He pointed at my plate.

"What*ever*!" I said in my best Valley Girl interpretation.

He had to go back to work, but not before kissing me thoroughly one more time. And he's coming back tonight. Even said he'd make dinner.

Now if I can just convince him that dessert won't kill me. Hmmmmm.

Eleven

Tuesday, 11 P.M.
Sweet, Texas
Witches with dirty thoughts: 1
Dead guys: 1 (But technically I didn't kill him)

Had an interesting phone call from London this afternoon. Callie said they were at the house in the city and she noticed some lurkies.

"The blokes stay about a block away. Long cloaks, weird eyes. This morning, I saw one of them walk past the house. And well," she laughed, "I killed him."

"What?" I choked on my bottled water. I'd been working out in the conservatory repotting some herbs that had outgrown their containers. It's amazing what moisture can do for a garden. When I'd come home from New York, so many of my plants were near death. Caleb and Kira had tried to do their best, but they don't have my witchy talent with the green things.

"Well, I used my powers to stop him. I tried to question him. He acted like he didn't know what I was doing but he did. The fear rolled off him." She took a deep breath.

Most witches are empaths, and can feel emotions. Few of us read minds the way I do, though. In fact, I'm the only one I know who does it.

"He passed out, or I thought he did. The autopsy said it was a heart attack. But I swear I didn't do anything but hold him." Callie's beautiful but kind of scary. No telling what she said to cause that guy cardiac arrest.

"I believe you. Did you call the spook squad?"

"Yes. There isn't any trouble, thanks to the prime minister and Zane. They told them about the attack in New York and of course they knew about your demon outside the pub. And they didn't find any other magic on him. He wasn't a warlock, he just wore these strange contacts."

I sat down on the kitchen stool by the island. "Did you happen to get a piece of clothing? Anything?"

"Yes. I threw it in the house before the spook squad got here. Why?"

I knew I liked her.

"We can use that material to trace where the magic is coming from and possibly track down the rest of that gang. He might not have been a warlock, but the people he hung out with definitely were." I took out a pen and paper from the drawer and wrote down a spell.

"Get the cloak and take it to your room. Oh, and grab some salt on the way."

"I'm not an idiot, Bronwyn." She snorted.

I didn't mean to insult her. It's very seldom I work with a witch who has the kind of power I do. There are only about seven of us right now, though that number is expected to triple in the next ten years.

Every few years, there's an influx of evil and our witch population grows out of need. It all happens sort of magically.

"Sorry, Callie. I'm so used to working with nonmagical folk. You know how it is."

She ignored the apology. People think I'm abrupt and cold at times, but she's tons worse.

A door creaked over the phone. "Okay, I'm in my room. I can't get into people's heads like you do, so how are we going to do this?" I could hear her shuffling around getting prepared.

"If you're up to it, I can use you as a conduit. You'll hold the cloth and see everything I do." I made some more notes.

"Wait, no, we can't do this," she interrupted. "Garnout said you shouldn't do magic for several weeks. It could kill you."

Damn, I'd actually forgotten. I only had four more days until the end of the week. And this wasn't so much magic, just using my ability to see into minds. I sometimes did it in my sleep by accident, so I figured it couldn't use that much power.

"I'm a lot better, really. And my magic moratorium is up in a few days, so let's do this."

I heard her shake the salt around the cloth. That would keep any black magic from spreading to Callie or me.

"Okay, but if you die in the middle of this I'm going to get really pissed off. And I'm telling Garnout it was your fault. Anything happens to you, I have a feeling my head wouldn't be long on my body." She was serious.

Garnout is always a bit overprotective of me, I don't know why. He likes me, I guess. Or maybe it's because I've saved some of his family members from terrible situations in the past. But I really don't need to know the reason: I'm just grateful he's my friend.

"Don't worry, Callie, I swear I'm stronger. And I'll be using your magic, not my own. Well, a little of mine. You'll see."

I told her the spell, and she chanted it three times while holding the cloth.

I closed my eyes and focused on her. I found her sitting in the room next to where I had stayed at Zane's. This one had yellow and blue polka dot paper. All of the furniture was white with yellow and blue accents.

Her hand clutched the cloak tight and I could feel her concentrating.

"I'm in your head, Cal." I said it softly but she still jumped.

"Cripes, that's fucking weird." Her voice was low and coarse.

"I know, I promise to be gentle. You'll feel a tingle in your hand. That's me, so don't freak and don't let go."

"Okay."

Taking a deep breath I focused her energy and mine on the material. Then I saw it. The back of a pub. A picture of a dog with a horse and rider. One of those hunting pictures the English are so fond of, and three men at a table. One of them argued with a man across the table.

"I don't know your fuckin' plan, but one of me mates just died. I say we kill the plonkers. All of 'em." The man was bald with a tattoo of an upside down cross on his forehead. People like that always make me think they should be wearing a sign advertising, Asshole Here, Kick My Ass Please.

"Me too," Callie whispered.

I'd forgotten that for the moment, reading minds went both ways. She could see into mine as easily as I did hers.

That meant I needed to keep mine on business.

I turned to see to whom he was talking, but a hood blocked the stranger's profile. Damn. Good news is, I could feel the location. Another man stood beside them. He too, was bald. Probably Nazi wannabes. But they had obviously been mixing with some dark magic warlocks.

"I agree." I heard Callie's voice in my head. She whispered, as if the men could hear us.

"Do you have the location?" I watched the men while I waited for her answer.

The other man spoke. "You'll kill no one until it's time. Your friend made a mistake. He didn't follow the plan, and that's why he's dead."

"Yeah, but you said your magic protected us. Made us invincible."

The man in the hood shook his head. "No, I told you that if you followed the plan, no one would die." He held up a long, withered hand. Reminded me of those creepy Halloween hands you buy at the costume shop—the ones with the fake blood dripping down. He was older than the others and his voice was rough as a gravel driveway.

"You'll do as I say. No more of this foolishness." He made a fist and hit the table.

Tattoo-guy looked defiant, and then bowed his head. "Yes, Master."

"Bronwyn," Callie interrupted. "I'm on it. Now out of my head, so I can go get the bastards."

I laughed. "Be careful, and call the spook squad. You've got a mix of warlock and stupid humans, never a good combination. You should have backup," I warned.

She snorted again. "You ever take backup?"

Had me there. "Fine, but be careful."

"Got it. And thanks. I've been itching to kill since I landed in this rainy hell."

It didn't rain much in Sydney, so London wasn't her favorite place.

Callie's special talent is throwing a green slime that knocks out bad guys. One whiff and he or she is out cold.

"Blessings," I said as I pulled back.

I opened my eyes to find Sam standing in front of me.

He took the phone from my hand and hung up.

I don't know why I held it. Callie and I had been speaking telepathically for the last few minutes.

His right eyebrow twitched, and I knew I was in for it.

"What the hell were you doing on the phone there? You were using magic, weren't you? I can't believe this. Do you have a death wish? Four days. You can't wait four days to use magic again?"

Man, he really loves me. I bit the inside of my lip to keep from smiling because I knew he wasn't in the mood for that kind of thing.

Stomping around the kitchen, he unloaded the two bags of groceries he brought in, slamming the fridge and cabinet doors.

Casper, who had finally come home to eat, ran out the pet door into the conservatory. She doesn't like yelling of any kind, unless she's the one mewling.

I know it's cruel, but the misters in the garden came on just at that moment. I took great joy in listening to her screech as she ran for the backyard. Serves her right for deserting me so much.

Sam sliced tomatoes, making loud chopping sounds as he did. My man was making me dinner even though he was thoroughly pissed. How sweet.

"I wasn't using my magic, Sam. I used Callie's." I stood, a little weak, but not bad. I had to build stamina. I walked up behind him and wrapped my arms around his waist, while he washed spinach leaves in the sink.

I breathed deeply and took in his scent. "She's going after the guys who sent the demon after me. All I did was help her locate them. A minimal amount of effort on my part."

He put the leaves on the counter and dried his hands on the towel. Turning, he put his hands on my shoulders as if to shake me.

Instead he kissed me. His energy soared through my body. I pressed into him, eager for more.

His eyes flashed open and he pulled me away from him. "Now *that* we are going to wait on until at least Friday." He smiled, taking the harshness from his words.

I slapped his chest playfully. "Oh, get over it. It's just sex, it's not like it's going to kill me."

"The way we do it, it could." He laughed, but his eyes were still serious. "You need to take it easy a couple of days, and you'll be surprised how much better you'll feel by Friday. But you can't use magic or have any of my incredible talents until the end of the week."

"Argh! This sucks." I knew he was right. Just the little bit of magic I did to help Callie had totally drained me, but I wasn't about to tell him.

"Go sit down. You're pale again, and I don't like it." He pushed me toward the table.

So much for keeping secrets.

He rattled on. "As much as Ms. Johnnie and Ms. Helen want to fatten you up, I think it wouldn't hurt to get some salad and maybe grilled chicken into you tonight. A healthy meal for once, and no more pie."

"That's just cruel. What do you mean no more pie? I'm skinnier than I've ever been. If I want pie I'm going to eat pie."

He chuckled. And then took a gold box out of one of the sacks.

"Are those Godiva truffles?" I sighed.

"Yes, but evidently I need to throw them in the trash because all you want is pie." He had the nerve to open the cabinet under the sink where I kept the trash.

"If you want to live, you'll stop right there and move that box slowly to the counter. Don't make me hurt you." I used my sexy voice. "And I will hurt you."

"Oooh. Now this could get fun. But I think I better just give you the chocolates so no one gets their heart rate up too high."

That made us both laugh.

I watched him preparing our meal. Everything seemed right.

We love each other so much and we have to make this work.

Now, I have to figure out how I can get him into my bed.

He's staked out my couch in front of the television. Said he didn't think it was a good idea for us to share a bed right now.

Stubborn man. And of course he'd have to be a doctor who knows all that crap about taking my pulse and listening for rasps in my chest.

Oh, and he made me drink this nasty herbal concoction Garnout told him would restore my strength. It works like the blue juice, but tastes like the bottom of an old shoe. Not that I've eaten a shoe, but I have a very good imagination.

Ooooh. I know. A massage.

"Hey Sam, um, I'm kind of tense. Could you rub my shoulders?"

Twelve

Sexually satisfied witches: 0 (Well, there are probably a few today but I'm not one of them)

My massage idea didn't work. Oh, Sam came up and rubbed my shoulders, right after he gave me some "special" tea. Friggin' tea knocked me out. The last thing I remember were his hands on my shoulders and me saying, "Oh, that feels . . ."

Argh!

You know, I happen to think being sexually frustrated isn't exactly healthy. And it's causing my blood pressure to raise a hell of lot more than if we actually did it.

There was an article on the Internet this morning about how a woman helped stop a gang from destroying a pub in London.

Of course, I heard the news firsthand when Callie called.

"Damn, what a rush." Callie had me on speaker while she soaked in the tub at Zane's country house. I could hear her sloshing around. It seemed kind of weird, but she called me, so there ya go.

"So, what happened? Did you get them all?" I sat on the couch with the television muted watching *The View*. I hate to admit it, but I'm kind of hooked on these morning talk shows. After *Good Morning America* there's Regis and Kelly, and then all of these women come on and talk about inane subjects and it's totally fascinating. And in the afternoon there's Ellen and Oprah. I'm now addicted to both shows. Well, not the Oprahs where murderers and rapists meet their victims. And ack the one where pedophiles talked about why they did what they did. It took everything I had not to mentally burn those idiots from the inside out. I may have to look them up someday.

But I love the celebrity interviews. It's silly, but after hanging out with Kira and Margie, I get into it now. Well, except when I'm the one hanging with the celebrity. But I like seeing how their homes are decorated and what kind of makeup they wear. There, I said it. Just please God don't tell Simone. She'll kick my ass. If the celebrity isn't fuckable, she's got no use for them.

"I didn't get them all," Callie grunted. "The old guy with the weird hands wasn't there. But cross-head was, along with four of his friends. Two were warlocks. I had to kill them all, so we didn't get much information."

Damn, she liked the violence part of the job way too much. Kind of like me. But we could have used some help getting to the source of the troubles.

"I have to tell you they were protected by some dark shit." Her husky voice sounded tired. "I haven't seen magic like that before. Hell, that one warlock, the one standing next to the guy in the booth, was a lot harder to kill than I expected. He threw this black sludge crap. Never seen anything like it."

I threw the remote on the coffee table. What the fuck? "Did you say black sludge?"

"God, Bronwyn, pay attention. Yes, why?"

I stood up and started pacing. "Did any of it get on you? Seep in anywhere?"

She laughed. "Hell, no. I'm fast on my feet. And that shit was nasty. I had a feeling it might take me down if it touched me, so I stayed clear."

I wish I had been so lucky. The last time I had a run-in with black sludge–spewing warlocks, they had been under Blackstock's control. I knew he wasn't the only one to use the stuff, but still.

"The spook squad did find some of the sludge on the wall behind the bar and took it in for testing. If they trace it anywhere I'll let you know."

We talked for a while longer about when I thought I could get back on the job. There's no way I'd have been able to fight like she did last night. I didn't have the strength, yet. And I honestly wasn't going to acquire it sitting around on my ass watching daytime television.

I still had a couple of days before it was safe to do magic, but I hadn't even so much as mixed a potion in almost two weeks.

I picked some herbs from the garden and got to work. I didn't do the magic over the charms, but did get them ready. After London, my supply was depleted. And I mixed energy, healing and protection potions, filling almost every available container I had.

I'm tired now and ready for lunch, but it's the good kind of tired. At least I accomplished something.

5 P.M.

Kira's coming over to exercise with me. Oh, geez. She's bringing a yoga DVD. She swears it will help me regain my strength and energy.

"I've been doing it for months, Bron, and I feel so much better. It's the one thing that's kept me from going crazy about this whole dead people thing." She called from the library. "It's all about breathing and stretching. It won't get your pulse up too high like something cardio, and I swear on a stack of Bibles you'll feel better when we're done."

"I don't know, Kira, it's so Hollywood." And it didn't sound very fun, though exercise seldom is.

"No, Bron, it's passé in Hollywood. Now everyone there is doing Pilates and something called Centering. Oh, I have a Pilates DVD too. I'll bring it. I do it twice a week and it's totally reshaped my butt."

I laughed. Kira was the last person to worry about body parts. She had a supermodel body and looks, a lawyer's analytical mind, and was honestly one of the kindest people I'd ever met.

So now I'm searching for my stretchy Juicy Couture shorts and a loose T-shirt for our little yoga spree.

Sam's got late rounds tonight but he promised to stop by later this evening. I have to find a way to get that man back into bed.

Thursday, 10 A.M.
Sweet, Texas
Witches who are clever: 1

What's the one thing a man can't turn down? I'm such a wickedly smart girl.

Sam walked in on Kira and me finishing our yoga DVD.

She was right about feeling better. I didn't think it would work the first time I tried it, but it did. I also like the idea of being more limber and centered. Garnout's always telling me I need to focus my power more. Yoga might help with that.

So Sam comes in the front door and we have our butts in the air in some downward dog thing. I turned to see him and he had one eyebrow up.

I pointed to him. "You stop looking at Kira's ass and get in the kitchen. We're almost done."

"No offense, Kira, but it's not your ass I'm interested in." He waggled his eyebrows and took the bags into the kitchen. Pots and pans were banged, so I assumed dinner wouldn't be long.

I love the fact that he cooks for me.

Kira had to get home to Caleb, who was also fixing dinner. Man, do we have these guys trained or what? He and Kira actually trade off each night, and do the same with household chores. They've become quite cozy since they met months ago.

So, Sam and I were alone in the kitchen. He was all about getting some steaks ready for the grill and baking potatoes. I mixed some more herbal iced tea. Gave him a kiss on the cheek, then ran upstairs for a quick shower.

That's when it dawned on me. I knew exactly what I needed to do. I tied a white T-shirt in a knot at my waist and pulled on a pair of loose pajama shorts. They have cute little pugs all over them and they are short.

Sam was bringing in the steaks.

They smelled heavenly.

We talked about his day at the hospital and then the nursing home. When we were done I grabbed the plates. I loaded the dishwasher and asked him to find a movie for us to watch.

"I'm kind of tired, Bron. I'm not sure I can make it through a whole movie tonight."

Oh, he was going to make it and then some.

"That's okay. We can always stop it and watch the rest to-morrow."

Honestly, I don't even know what movie he chose. I was so focused on what I was about to do, I didn't even look. I brought in our tea, and set it on the coffee table.

He put his arm around me when I sat down. I nuzzled his neck and the smell of him gave me courage. I put my hand on his thigh and rubbed gently. Closed my eyes and sighed. That's when my hand accidentally moved upward. He instantly hardened under my palm. Oops.

"Bron?"

"Yes?"

"What are you doing?" He shifted on the couch, but he didn't stop me.

"I'm getting dessert ready." I got down on my knees and smiled up at him.

"Honey, you know we can't. It's just a few more days."

I pushed his legs apart and undid his jeans one button at a time. "Baby, you can wait all you want. I'm going down on you. Now."

I bent down and took him in my mouth. He grew even harder.

He groaned and put his hands in my hair. "We can't—oooh . . ."

I smiled around him and then sucked hard. He felt so good in my mouth, the taste of him.

He moaned again, and I licked and sucked and could hear his breath become a pant.

"Jesus, woman. You've got to stop. I can't hold out much longer."

Silly man, that was the point.

I did pause for a second and looked at him. Don't know what he saw in my eyes, but he whispered, "Okay."

His hips moved in motion, and just before I knew he was about to come, I slid back to his tip.

He grabbed my shoulders and pulled me up to him and kissed me. His hardness pressed between us.

Then he pushed me away. "Stand up, Bronwyn."

I did what he asked, afraid he was going to stop the game.

He tugged my shorts down my legs. Smiling when he saw I wore nothing underneath. Pulling me up on the couch so that I was standing over him. Then he plunged his tongue between my legs. I had to grab the back of the couch to keep from falling. His tongue slid in and out and my body shook with pleasure seconds later. I came so hard I thought I would pass out.

Sam slid out from underneath me and brought my feet back to the floor. Standing behind me, he bent me over the couch. My hands held on to the back, as he slid into me.

I moaned when he grabbed my tits and plunged deeper into me. Pounding me harder and harder.

I screamed, this time my whole body trembling.

"Saammm. Yesssss."

He didn't stop, just moved in and out to the point where I felt like my whole body would come to pieces. Not in a painful way, but in a glorious shiver of pleasure.

When he came he moaned, "Bron." And I collapsed back onto him, reaching for his head and pulling him to me. He kissed the back of my neck and then slid tiny kisses down my spine.

I turned to him and he kissed me again, this time, our tongues playing that timeless game.

Then he grabbed my wrist and, looking at his watch, he took my pulse.

I yanked at him. "Stop that. I'm fine. In fact I feel better than I have in weeks."

"You're doing okay. I just wanted to make sure."

I looked down at us. We both had our shirts on and no bottoms. I reached down and grabbed the clothes. He pulled me upstairs and we had a repeat performance in the shower, after a few minutes of playing hide the soap.

A blow job. It works every time.

Thirteen

The local coven is coming over tonight. It's the first time I'm going to try real magic after a couple of weeks off, so they'll be here as kind of a fail-safe.

It's Garnout's idea. He's fond of the local witches and warlocks in town. They keep Sweet running smoothly, and force trouble away with their protection spells. It's one of the safest places I've ever lived.

We did have that problem with Blackstock a few months ago, but he'd slid in under the guise of another warlock, Cole. It was ironic since Cole is one of the bigwigs of the international spook squad. He almost died too, with me in the conservatory. If he hadn't given me some of his healing power I wouldn't be writing this down right now.

So, Garnout says it's best to have some magical folk around in case something goes wrong.

Ms. Peggy is the leader of the coven. In a small world kind of way, she and my mom actually went to college together. I've become a surrogate daughter ever since we found that out.

She and Mom had lost touch, but now they talk all the time. Goodie for me. Argh. I seem to be a favorite topic of their conversations.

The rest of the coven is made up of a mix of Wiccans, most of whom aren't that powerful. But there are a few that can hold their own. Like Janet. She's strong and so is her boyfriend, Mike. I'm not overly fond of warlocks, well, except for Sam, of course, but he doesn't practice. Mike does practice, but he's a clean soul. I've even probed his mind a few times to make sure there's no darkness hiding in there.

Speaking of cleaning, I'm running around the house trying to get it ready.

My energy level is higher than it's been in forever. I woke up this morning with so much excitement, after a night of mind-blowing sex, and I'm so ready to throw some fireballs.

I'm going to start small and work my way up. It's as if my body knows. Before I had my shower this morning, my mind traveled to check on the prime minister, Zane, Azir and my friend Simone. It's something I usually do on a regular basis, without even thinking about it.

Azir was asleep, so not much going on there. The prime minister was in a meeting. Go figure. Zane was working in the studio again. And Simone was just coming in from a very late night out.

Since I knew she was up, I called. She'd been checking on me every day, and had left a message last night. I couldn't answer. I was kind of tied up. With scarves on the bedpost and whipped cream from head to toe. . . . No, can't think about that right now.

Simone picked up on the first ring.

"Hey, are you okay?" Thanks to caller ID she never bothers with greetings.

"I'm good. Tonight's the first time to try magic after a few weeks. I kind of hope I don't blow up my house."

She laughed. "You know you won't. In fact I talked to Garnout, and he thinks you'll be more powerful and focused than ever since you've been conserving energy."

What is it with everyone gossiping about me behind my back? Garnout's talking to my mom, Sam and now Simone. Geez.

"Well, we'll see what happens tonight. I'm not quite a hundred percent but I'm close." I grabbed the dustcloth and started in on my dining room table and chairs. For some reason, that room gets dustier faster than any other in the house.

"I still think you should come out here and hang with me. The sea air would do you good." Simone lives in the middle of Hollywood, but she does love the beach. "We could do all that girly crap. Spa treatments, nails and highlights with the master stylist Sir David."

Honestly, it sounded like fun. I hadn't taken a real vacation in more than three years, and the last one to Bermuda was interrupted by a warlock attack. I came home with a wicked sunburn and three more kills.

"I'll think about it. For real, Simone. But I'm not up to travel-ing quite yet. And when I am, I've got to get back on the job. Cal-lie can't cover for me forever."

"Callie the Bitch is covering for you in London?"

I laughed. Did I mention that Simone doesn't have many friends? She doesn't care for most people. The fact that we are friends often amazes me.

"Yes, and she's been doing a great job. Okay, so she's not the friendliest person, but neither are you." I laughed.

"You've got me there. I just figured the probabilities of you coming out in the next month and it's seventy-eight to one. Not good odds."

We never say it to her face but our nickname for Simone is Rain Man. She's a fucking genius with numbers. I mean for real. The cool thing is she doesn't look like a math nerd. She's got co-coa skin, long straight dark hair and she's tall. Legs up to her shoulders.

"Well, you never know." I moved my dusting to the living room.

"Man, Bron, I've gotta crash. We had a demon infestation in Topanga. I took out the nest, but it's been a twenty-four-hour mission." The tiredness in her voice was evident.

"Sorry, girl. I should have known better than to call you be-fore noon."

"Hell, don't worry about it. I'd just walked in the house. But call me later tonight or tomorrow and let me know what hap-pens with your magic practice. Wish I could be there."

I finished cleaning and ate a sandwich for lunch. Sam had to drive into Dallas to consult one of his patients who had moved there. He'd probably stay overnight, which was actually good.

He felt awkward around a lot of the coven because they had helped to save his life. And with him around it would be more difficult to focus.

Oh wow. I'm kind of nervous and excited. But I need to rest.

Saturday, 8 A.M.
Sweet, Texas
Rockin' witches: 14
Insane wizards: 1

I love the women and men who make up the coven in Sweet. They are like family, or are quickly becoming so.

Everyone brought food last night and it turned into a big potluck. Well, a big potluck with lots of chanting and burned paper plates.

They all showed up around seven loaded down with everything from tacos to strawberry shortcake. We set it up in the dining room and along the long counter in the kitchen.

It was the first time I'd had them all in the house at the same time. A few had come to visit off and on, and some, like Janet, had been here when Blackstock attacked me in the conservatory.

After we ate, everyone headed to the backyard. I have sod for about an acre, but the other ten acres are dry West Texas land. Lots of scrub and dirt. We walked to the area where the grass ended. Caleb had raked the area so that it was mostly smooth dirt.

They set up a circle around me and chanted a protection spell.

I didn't know how this first bit would go, but I brought up a tiny fireball in the air just above my right hand. The hard part is sustaining, so I focused. It didn't take any effort, so I tossed it in the air.

That gave Mike the idea for me to try and hit a moving target.

"Are you volunteering?" I laughed, my voice a little edgy from nerves.

"No, but I thought maybe we could toss these up and you could try and hit them." He pulled out a package of paper plates, and I heard gales of laughter from the other witches and warlocks.

He shrugged. "Well we can toss 'em up and see what happens." Embarrassed, he smiled.

"It's a great idea. Go ahead."

He threw the first one like a Frisbee. Just as it was about to land on Peggy's head, I blew it to bits. She stepped back. "Mike," she yelled shrilly, "you throw those darn things close to me again, and you'll have a skunk's tail by morning."

My shoulders shook with laughter but I didn't let the giggles escape. Several other people did the same.

Mike shrugged. "Sorry, Peg, I'll toss them outside the circle this time."

He threw two at once and, without thinking, I disintegrated them.

"Keep the circle, but everyone move back about ten paces." I motioned them out with my hands. "That's good. Don't freak out. I want to try something."

I pointed with my finger to the ground and, in a matter of seconds, I had a circle of fire three feet away surrounding me, burning about knee high.

The faces of the coven were bright with wonder. Their expressions made me smile. I extinguished the circle.

"She'll never have to worry about being on a deserted island without matches," Mavis Calright, a nervous Wiccan, whispered.

She was a nice lady, but even though she looked like Jackie O, Mavis had foot-in-mouth disease. I liked her. She always made me laugh.

Enough with the child's play. Taking a breath, I lifted my hands to the sky.

Mother Earth, share your bounty,
Mother Sky, let me feel your breath.
As I will so mote it be.

Under our feet a mat of grass grew from the dry dirt. And wind picked up, cooling the August heat that had left a sheen on many a nose and forehead in the circle.

The breeze whipped around us, lifting skirts and sending hats sailing through the air, but no one broke the circle.

Another deep breath and I brought my arms down. The grass stayed, but the wind died down.

"Crap, Bron, you're even stronger than before." That was Janet.

What she didn't know is that I could have done so much more.

Just then the wind picked up, but only in the center of the circle. I had nothing to do with it.

In popped Garnout. His long white beard had been braided. He wore a tie-dyed shirt and jeans. In the six years I've known him, I'd never seen him in anything but wizard robes.

"Welcome." I smiled.

"I felt your power and came to make sure you were doing okay. You look pale." He stepped toward me and stopped, then stared at me strangely.

I looked down at my clothes. I wore jeans, and a pink T-shirt

Sam had given me. It said, Humanity Is Overrated. I used to hate pink but it's sort of grown on me. I didn't see anything out of order.

"It's coming," he whispered as he walked around me in a circle.

"What's coming?" I looked behind me. I didn't see anything.

"More." He said it without inflection.

Reaching out, he touched my shoulder. "No more tonight. You need to rest. Build each day. More is to come."

Before I could ask again what "more" meant, he disappeared. The coven members whispered around me.

I turned to Janet. "Any idea what he's talking about?"

She shrugged. "Not a clue, but he's right. You look pale. Let's go back in and grab a snack."

They joined hands and chanted healing and clearing of magic spells. The grass underneath us disappeared.

The coven left a little later, and a short time after that, I was asleep.

Sam should be home in a few hours. He called from Dallas, but he didn't sound like he was in a good mood. I hope his patient is okay.

I'm heading to the Piggly Wiggly to stock up on Hershey's syrup. A girl can never have too much chocolate, especially when it's drizzled all over her man.

Fourteen

Saturday, 11 P.M.
Sweet, Texas
Spells: 4
Charms: 5
Cranky witches: 1

It's been good to use magic again. Unlike everyone around me, I think if I don't do a little each day it builds up in my system and makes me weaker. I'll probably never convince anyone of that but myself, but I won't go so long without using it in the future. Don't care what anyone says.

And what the hell did Garnout mean about "more"? He's so cagey. I've e-mailed him twice and he wrote, "You'll know soon enough."

Geez. Of course I shouldn't take my bad mood out on my wizard buddy, but still.

So, this is something I've been curious about for a long time. Why is it I can only be happy for a maximum of two days before some drama rises up and saps all the good out of the day? I'd really like someone in the universe to explain it to me.

Sam showed up around noon today. I had run into town to get some avocado sandwiches from Lulu's. The new bakery, Milly's, had some beautiful cakes in the window and I couldn't resist the Black Forest.

Had everything set up and ready to go for Sam. I knew he was tired. I could hear it in his voice when he called from the road. Also had my Hershey's chocolate nearby, just in case.

When he came in, his forehead was etched with stress. There was a lot more than a long drive and a difficult medical case in the worry in his eyes.

"What happened?" I didn't pretend not to notice his mood.

"Nothing, I told you it's a difficult case and we can't seem to agree on a treatment." He sat down and took a bite of his sandwich.

If I had half a brain, I would have let it go. Whatever was really wrong, he wasn't ready to talk about it. But no, Bronwyn can never let anything rest. I've got to push and needle until the other person explodes.

I crossed my arms and stared at him.

He threw his fork down on the plate, and shook his head. "Leave it be, Bron. I'm not in the mood for your games."

Now that just pissed me off.

"What do you mean *games*? I don't play games with you, Sam. Something's bothering you, and I want to help. How is that messing with your mind? Please explain it to me." I could feel my lips pressing into a line, and I bit the inside of my cheek to keep from saying something I would regret.

He stood up and pushed his chair in. "I can't do this right now." And he walked out.

Just like that. Stupid jerk. There isn't anything he can't tell me. He should know that by now.

I thought about using my powers to stop him, but decided against it. Screw it. This relationship crap is too hard. I mean it. I'm so tired of the drama.

And I'm friggin' trying this time. I really am. I wish I could just say, "Fuck it," but I can't. I hurt for him and I know something's not right. Stupid asshole.

Sunday, 9 A.M.
Confused witches: I
At one this morning Sam slipped into my bed. Scared the crap out of me at first. I didn't even hear him come in. No one could get past my protection wards but friends and family, but it did shock me to suddenly feel someone on the other side of the bed.

I cracked an eye and saw him lying on his side staring at me.

"Hey," I whispered.

"Hey." He reached out and pushed the hair off of my face. "I'm sorry about before."

Pulling me to him, he rubbed my back.

I took a deep breath and inhaled him. Sandalwood and patchouli, he never disappoints. "It's okay."

"No, it's not. I just needed some more time. I thought I could push it aside but I couldn't. I don't think I'm as over things as I thought." The last was said on a whisper.

I pulled away. "What are you talking about?"

"My ex, she was at the hospital with her husband." He took my hand and rubbed my fingers. "We all pretended like there was nothing awkward about it. They were in town for a friend's engagement party, and stopped by the hospital to see some of his former colleagues. I told them to have a nice visit and went on to my patient." He sat up and leaned against the headboard, but he didn't let go of my hand.

"Did seeing her trigger all of the old memories? Do you still have feelings for her?" Sam came with some baggage. He'd found his ex-fiancée in bed with two of his best friends the night before they were supposed to get married. Well, they were former best friends now. His trust issues had a strong foundation in doubt. I've known it from the beginning and, since I share a lot of the same kind of trust issues, I figure we're perfect for one another.

"God, no." He snorted. "I can barely stand being in the room with her. She makes my skin crawl."

"Then what happened to put you in such an awful mood?"

He kissed my fingertips. "I am really sorry for taking it out on you."

"And I told you it's okay, but tell me why."

"Well, a couple of hours later I was coming out of the patient's hospital room, and she stood there waiting for me. She said she wanted to talk to me and it would only take a few minutes." He frowned.

I nodded, encouraging him on.

"I didn't want to talk to her. Honestly, it makes me ill to be near her now. But I took her to a friend's office. He wasn't there and it was private. That's when—crap. It makes me sick to say it." Sam paused.

In that moment my heart sank to my toes. If he did anything with her, I'm not at all sure I could be a grown-up about it. Really. I could feel my temper rising. I shoved everything back down.

He stared ahead in the dark. The light from the moon outside highlighted his profile. "She told me she was pregnant."

My heart went from my toes to my throat. No, no, the timing was wrong. He hadn't seen her in more than six months. She'd sent him an invitation to her wedding, but a warlock had almost killed him, so he had a good excuse for not going.

"She said she wished the baby was mine. That she was sorry for what she did and that she still loved me." He turned to me. "What kind of woman is pregnant with another man's child and says something like that?"

A fucked-up one. I didn't say anything, but if I ever met this woman she would walk away with an ass four times her normal size and a couple of warts on her nose. I kissed his fingers like he did mine.

"I wanted to hit her, Bron. I've never wanted to hit a woman. Ever. Especially, a pregnant woman. But she made me sick. Her words made me physically ill."

Me too.

"So what did you say?" I moved closer and put my head on his chest, wrapping my arms around his waist. He needed comfort.

"I told her she was sick and that she needed to find a good psychiatrist." He laughed. "She looked like I had hit her. I said if she ever came near me again, I'd tell her husband everything.

"It isn't right, or fair, but on the way home, all those thoughts about you and that Zane guy came up. When I walked in and saw you, I kept thinking, *Will she do the same thing? Can I trust anyone?* Just a few months ago you couldn't decide between Azir and me. Is what we have real?

"I was driving myself crazy at home and then I realized something. I love you so much. If there's any chance of making this thing work, I've got to let the past go."

I squeezed him tighter. "I love you too. Only you. I don't blame you for being upset about Zane, but rest assured I have absolutely no feelings for him other than as a client. He's charming and a good friend. That's it."

Sam kissed me hard. "God, Bron. I can't stand the idea of losing you."

"You aren't going to lose me. I'm in for the long haul." I kissed him back.

We ended up making love. It was tender, maybe not as passionate as the last time, but good. The thing is, I noticed that when our auras mixed this time, something was off. When we climax there's usually a golden haze, but this was almost amber. Kind of orangey. It wouldn't be a big deal, except for what happened at about five this morning.

Sam's cell phone rang. I turned over, figuring it was the hospital or nursing home calling him in. That's a doctor's life.

But the conversation was weird.

"Yes," Sam answered. "What time? I've got to run and get my things and I'll be there." Then he hung up.

He reached over and kissed me. "I've got to go out of the country for a few days. I'll call when I get back." Then he went to the bathroom before I could say anything.

I sat up and grabbed his phone. Pushing the buttons I found the number of whoever had called him. I didn't recognize it. I heard him coming out and put the phone back on the nightstand.

Reaching for him, I grabbed his hand. "Did you say out of the country? Where?"

He kissed me again, this time on the forehead. "Sorry, babe. Can't tell you. You're not the only one who has secrets about the job." Pulling on his pants, he had the nerve to smile like it was some kind of joke.

"Wait a minute, why would you have to leave the country for your job?" It was a valid question. He's a small town doctor. It didn't make sense.

He shook his head. "I mean it, I can't say. If I can, I'll tell you when I get back. I may be out of touch for a while. I don't know what kind of reach I'll get with my cell phone." He hugged me. "I love you."

Then the big jerk just walked out. Maybe it was the early hour, but I didn't take it well.

When the door slammed downstairs I heard him turn the key. He'd gone.

I let my frustration out in a primal scream that shook the house. For real. The ground moved. I sat in the middle of the bed on my knees and looked around. Two pictures had fallen off the wall and several knickknacks on the dresser had toppled.

What was that?

I tried to see if I could do it again, but nothing happened. Then I thought about how angry I was with Sam. The stupid jerk. We'd just made up. He couldn't run off to another country without any kind of explanation. That was my MO.

I pounded the bed with my fist and the house shook again. Now, it could have been an earthquake, but since we live on zero fault lines, I found that hard to accept.

Turns out I have a new power. I can shake the earth.

I waited an hour and called Garnout. Excited about the new power, and still kind of pissed at Sam, I told the wizard what happened with the earthquake.

"There you have it. More." He laughed.

"So, you knew I was about to get a new power?"

"Yes, but I didn't know how it would manifest or when."

I moved down to the kitchen and made a pot of orange and cinnamon tea. "Not that I'm not grateful, but what good is something like this?"

He laughed hard this time. "Why, to keep your enemies off balance, my dear. Learn to focus on that power and you'll soon discover it comes in quite handy."

Other than informing me that I needed to meditate more and learn to sustain the energy, he didn't have much else to say.

So I'm going to try yoga again, and then some meditation. And I'm not going to think about Sam and his quick exit this morning because that makes me very angry. Damn, just shook the teacup off the counter. What a mess.

Fifteen

Monday, 2 P.M.
Sweet, Texas
Spells: 1
Snoopy witches: 1

When your troubles weigh heavy, ask a friend about hers. It always makes you feel better. It's sad, but true.

Poor Kira, she's in a tizzy. The dead people won't leave her alone. I had to get out of the house and away from my own thoughts.

Sam left a message while I was in the shower. "Sorry again about the rush this morning. But it's all good, we'll talk when I get home." I promised him months ago to never pry into his mind or try and locate him. But well, I just did a quick flash and saw he was on a jet. It looked like a private one.

He does a lot of work with his father, who is a big humanitarian, so I wondered if that had something to do with it.

Like I said, had to get out of the house and away from my own head.

Stopped by the library and, it being a Monday, no one was there. It was one of her slowest days of the week, but Kira seemed a bit more flustered than normal.

Dressed in a black Armani pinstriped suit, four-inch Pradas and her long blond curls hanging loose around her shoulders, she couldn't have looked less like a small town librarian. She'd made a small fortune during her tenure as a corporate lawyer, and spent a good portion of it on her clothes. You can take the girl out of the big city, but not necessarily away from her favorite designers.

"So, bad day?"

She shoved her curls behind her ears. "I've had it up to here with these damn ghosts." She put her hand to the top of her forehead.

"What happened?" I picked up a book and handed it to her to stack on the shelf in front her.

"They want me to help them. Now I don't just see them, I hear them. And—"

She rolled her eyes. "The worst was this morning. Mrs. Archer, the one who owns that big ranch out south, came in to return some books. There was this old man who walked up to the desk right before and was asking if we had anything on World War II. I told him to check the back wall far right corner where we keep most of the historical novels. Mrs. Archer looked at me like I had three heads."

Kira stepped over to another shelf and pulled the book cart

with her. Normally she treats books like small treasures, but she was slamming them into the shelves.

"I asked her if I could help her, and she kept staring. 'Excuse me, Mrs. Archer can I help you?' I said it again. She handed me her books and then she said, 'Who were you talking to before?' 'I don't know his name,' I told her. She patted my hand. 'Dear, are you feeling well? There wasn't anyone there. You were talking to thin air.'

"I almost passed out right then and there. I'd been conversing with a ghost. When I looked at the corner where I'd sent him, no one was there. I said something stupid like I must have been daydreaming. I'm sure now the whole town knows the librarian's off her rocker. But he seemed so real, Bron."

I handed her another book. "Don't beat yourself up, girl. This is all new to you, but you'll learn how to tell the dead from the living. I know. How about I teach you to see auras? Dead people don't have auras, so that way you can tell."

She turned to face me. "Do you think I could learn to do that?"

"Sure. Trust me, it's a lot harder to see dead people than it is auras. Since you can already read different energies, it'll probably be even easier. Why don't you come to the house tonight? Have you told Caleb yet?"

She frowned. "No, the right time hasn't come up. Though I'm sure he thinks something is up because he heard me talking to myself in the bathroom the other morning." She made a face. "Well, I was talking to the dead people. But he's back in New York this week working on that story, so I'm free. Do you think I can do this?"

I laughed. "Yes, you can. And I wish you wouldn't worry so much about telling Caleb. He's a big toad, but he loves you and he hangs with me, so he understands the metaphysical world better than most men do."

She smiled and held one of the books to her chest. "Yes, he'll probably be great about it. But I think I have to accept it first."

I made a few more stops, one of which included peeking into Janet and Mike's new bookstore. They were set to open in a few weeks, and it was looking good. Cherry wood bookcases lined the walls. There were short aisles of shelves and some tables for displays. They hadn't revealed the name yet. The sign over the door was wrapped in brown paper. I didn't see either of them, so I decided to head out and check on the jet.

Caleb had flown her home from New York for me, but I always like to check her out before and after flights. It'd probably be another few days before I should fly. But I could hardly wait. I love to fly. It's one of the few times in my life I can let go of everything except concentrating on the task.

Darryl was in his office. He runs the Sweet airport, and he waved while he talked on the phone.

My girl looked good. Azir had given her to me right after we first met. I'd tried to give the jet back several times, but he wouldn't have it. The PM is the one who finally convinced me to keep it.

She's glorious, with rich leather interior for the sofas and chairs. A gold-plated bathroom. It's the most ostentatious thing I've ever owned. And I missed it so much.

By the time I got home, I had four messages on my phone. The first was the prime minister asking me to call him back as soon as possible. The second was from Zane, with the same message. The third and fourth were from Miles basically asking the same thing, but not as nice.

"If you're so damn sick, where the hell are you?" Miles mumbled. "Your expertise is needed." And he hung up.

I rang the prime minister's direct line in hopes of bypassing snippy little Miles. It worked.

"Hello, Prime Minister."

"Hello, Bronwyn, how are you feeling?" He was always so polite.

"I'm much better, thank you." It was the truth. It'd been almost three weeks since the attack, and I felt stronger than ever.

"Do you think you might be ready for a new assignment in a week or so?"

Wow. Hadn't really planned to go back for another two weeks. I wanted to work, but I wasn't sure my body was up to it.

"I wouldn't ask so soon, but I need your help with Zane."

"Did something happen?" I realized I hadn't called to check in with Callie for a couple of days. The last time she spoke things had been quiet, and she promised to let me know if the spook squad got anything from the black sludge at the pub.

Usually I did mental checks on Azir and the PM on a daily basis. I hadn't been able to use my magic in so long, I'd gotten out of practice.

"No, it's just that he has to come that way to prepare for his new concert and Callie has to return to Australia. Seems there's a problem only she can deal with and they need her back."

"So do you need me to come to London on Friday?"

"No, this one is a bit closer to home for you. Zane is preparing for the new tour and it begins in Los Angeles. Would it be possible for you to meet him there at the end of the week?"

I thought about it for a few seconds. By the end of the week I'd be even better than I was now. I still get tired, but I'd been tired before on assignments and managed.

"When does his plane get in?"

"He's scheduled for noon. I haven't told him any of this. He seems to think that since Callie took care of those warlocks the threat is over, but I have a feeling it's only just begun."

"Why do you think that sir, if you don't mind my asking?" I moved around the office shuffling papers. I'd really let things stack up while I was sick.

"Just a feeling. Aren't you the one who always tells me to follow my instincts where threats are concerned?"

"Yes, that sounds like me. Okay, I can't be there before noon. Garnout has to check me out on Friday morning before I can leave. He wants it to be a full three weeks. But I'll have Simone, my friend the demon slayer, meet Zane. She'll take him to his home. I'll be there a couple of hours after."

"That's acceptable. Simone? Have I met her?" He sounded distracted.

"Trust me sir, if you'd met her, you'd remember. But she knows Zane. She's the one he asked about in New York."

"Oh yes, that's where I remember the name. I'll have Miles send the itinerary when we have it complete."

"Yes, sir."

"And Bronwyn, thank you. Sheik Azir and I will meet you there by the end of the second week."

"What?" I tried to ask, but he'd hung up.

I sighed. I have to build my stamina, my resistance to Azir, learn to use my new power and get myself into fighting shape in just one week.

That's when it dawned on me. I pulled my iPod out of my purse to check the addresses and phone numbers. Sure enough, there it was. The number on Sam's cell phone. It was Azir who had called him out of my bed.

I couldn't imagine any scenario other than Azir had asked for help with one of his humanitarian missions. It's noble of them both, but if Azir gets Sam killed, I'll have to hurt him in return.

It also explains why Sam acted so strange that morning. Whenever Azir is involved in any of our conversations things tend to get weird.

So they were off saving people. Azir does it all the time. He pulls women and children out of atrocious circumstances and gives them better lives.

I'd had a chance to meet a few of the women he'd saved when I visited his home in Dubai. They nearly worshipped the man for all he had given them. Their stories . . . well, that those women hadn't lost their faith in humanity was some small miracle.

Okay, so Sam's off saving the world. I do it all the time. I guess I have to give the guy a break.

9 P.M.

Kira's a friggin' genius. I swear she learns faster than anyone I've ever seen in my life. Well, with the exception of Simone.

Within an hour of showing her how to look but not look—that's the secret of aura reading—she was doing it. She could even see Casper's aura. And animals are lot more difficult than people.

We drove into town and sat in Lulu's eating chocolate cream pie. (I swear I'll start eating healthy tomorrow.) She read every single patron correctly. Amazing.

I don't know how I ended up with all of these brilliant friends, but I'm feeling a bit blessed today.

The good news is she's beginning to accept her gifts as a talent and not so much a curse. I explained that these things come to us for a purpose, and she'll soon discover what that is.

I dropped her back at her house.

She reached over and hugged me. "Thank you for being my friend." She smiled. "For the first time in weeks I don't feel like I have a hundred pound weight sitting on my shoulders. I can breathe."

"Thank you. I don't know what I would have done without you and Caleb these last few weeks."

It was just a big old lovefest and we both got a little teary-eyed.

She sniffled. "So tomorrow after work I'll come over and we'll do yoga and we'll work on the meditation thing. Then I'll watch while you practice making earthquakes."

I waved as she got out the door. "Sounds like a plan. See ya tomorrow."

Now, if Sam would call and let me know he's alive and well, this would be a great day. Not going to happen, but a girl can wish.

Sixteen

Saturday, noon
Beverly Hills, California
Drugged, pissed-off witches: 1

Whoohoo! I love L.A. Yep, been here twenty-four hours and so far I've slept twenty-three of them. Oh, and in the first half hour I was shot.

Okay, it was a tranquilizer gun, but still. Come on.

Garnout wouldn't let me take my own plane. He was worried about my power suddenly jumping out and making me crash or something. I'm also not exactly feeling my best. I was so much better until yesterday.

Caleb was still in New York, so I had to take a commercial flight. I get off the plane and since I flew into Burbank, you disembark outside. Being the lucky person that I am, I was shot by a tranq dart meant for some demon, in a human disguise. He was on my plane, but hadn't caused any trouble. The spook squad was after him and they hit me and three others, totally missing the demon, according to Simone.

She and Zane were waiting just outside baggage claim for me with the limo. When the demon came out, she captured him. When I didn't make it out, they sent security to find me. Long story short, they found me in the on-site medical facility, passed out.

I woke up about a half hour ago to find myself inside a bedroom decorated in gold and sapphire blue. Not me, but very elegant.

Turns out it's another of Zane's mansions. He and Simone had been waiting for me to wake up.

I found them downstairs in the kitchen eating lunch.

"Oh, look it's a witch." Zane did a fake scream.

"Cute." I poked him in the shoulder.

"What the hell happened to me?" I grabbed a roll and sat down in the huge breakfast room. Everything was white and black down here. A Zen kitchen and breakfast room. Only in L.A.

They told me the story about the demon and I rolled my eyes. "God, only I could be accidentally shot by a spook squad."

"Well, to be fair, Bron, you send off magic like a crazy person, even when you aren't trying to. I can see why they would get confused." Simone shrugged.

"Hey, you're supposed to be on my side, demon slayer."

She laughed. "Don't get all witchy on me, I am on your side. So, look, I've got appointments tomorrow for both of us with Sir David. And then we are going to Maxie to get our eyebrows done."

She stood and pushed in her chair. Dressed in a skimpy green T-shirt and low-cut jeans so tight I didn't see how she could breathe, she looked like an Amazon princess. I've always been a little envious of her height, natural tan and incredibly straight hair. But I would never in this lifetime tell her that.

She walked around the table and hugged me. "I'm so glad you're here. We're going to have fun, but right now I have to stop by the university to run some numbers, then I'm off to find a demon nest in Huntington Beach. These assholes have been terrorizing swimmers for a week." She pushed on her sunglasses and headed out the door.

Zane sipped his wine. "Did she say university? I didn't think she taught anymore."

It surprised me that he knew so much about her. Simone's good about keeping her lives separate and secret. Her main job is as a demon slayer, but as I said before, she's brilliant with the math. She is Rain Man.

"She doesn't teach, but she's got a bunch of students helping her with research. Of course they have no idea she's having them search for demon nests."

Zane laughed, then turned serious. "I'm glad you're feeling better. I don't think I've ever been so frightened as when you passed out in the kitchen in London. I thought you died. Matt whipped out his phone, but before he could dial, that wizard was there and whisked you away. I'd never seen anything like it. I'm sorry your illness was caused by the demon that attacked us. I feel like all of this is my fault."

I reached across and patted his arm. "Don't worry about it. Honestly, it's a part of the job. If it hadn't been that situation it would have been another one." I yawned. I needed a shower, a serious meal and to rest just awhile longer.

"Let me get you something to eat." It was as if he read my mind.

I waved him away. "Sit down. I'll get it." And I did. The fridge was packed with lots of healthy choices. Fruit, fresh vegetables and about a hundred bottles of Fiji water. I went for the chocolate pudding and frozen White Castle burgers I found. Popped the burgers in the microwave and put them on a fancy china plate with black and white checks. If you stared too long, it would make you dizzy. The pudding went in a bowl with the same pattern.

Zane was at the table talking on his cell phone. I plopped down and dug in. The food tasted so good. I ate about six burgers before I looked up and saw Zane watching me.

"How do you stay so tiny when you eat such an atrocious diet?" He made a weird frowny face. "My God, woman, pudding and hamburgers."

I threw up my hands. "I was hungry, what's the big deal?"

"Most of the time when someone is trying to feel better they eat a diet rich in fruits and vegetables. If I ate like you I'd crash and burn onstage. I'd never build any kind of stamina or strength."

"Hey, you build your stamina your way, I'll build it mine. It's carbs, protein." I held up the bowl of pudding. "And dairy. Not a damn thing wrong with it."

He grimaced again. "I've got to meet the guys in the studio out back. Why don't you come around a little later?"

"Okay. Hey, I thought you said Zoë was going to travel with you for a while."

He turned back from the door and smiled. "She is, but she wants to finish out the school year. I promised we could hire a tutor, but she really wanted to stay. I know she's lonely, but I don't know what else to do."

I smiled at him. He really was trying. "I'm sure she's fine."

The day I met her was still a bit of a blur. It was just a few hours after that I'd passed out in Zane's kitchen. There was something about her, something I'd wanted to tell him when we were alone, but I couldn't remember what it was.

Oh well. I rinsed the dishes and put them in one of the two dishwashers. Then I came back up here for a shower. The sad thing is, I could take another nap. Damn dart. But I need to get back on Zane's case.

A little meditation might help me recharge. It's so hard for me to sit still and clear my mind, but I need to do it right now.

Saturday, 4 P.M.

I visited the studio out back. It's past the pool and down a little path through the gardens. This place is so big, you get lost. I did twice, just taking the wrong paths off of the pool. There's like six of them. One goes to the studio, another goes to a guesthouse, one to the front of the house and I don't know about the others. I finally found the studio on the third try.

Zane and the band were working hard, and I always feel like such an outsider. I decided to head back in and see if I could do a little mental work on his case.

First I wanted to check on little Zoë. After watching her mourn for her parents, it wasn't such a happy prospect tapping into her again.

It was late in the evening but she was awake. She looked up at the ceiling and said, "Hello."

Took me a minute to realize she was talking to me. She could see me in her mind, but projected it out. Interesting. Then I remembered. It was the magic. I wanted to research her birth mother to see if she'd been a witch.

"Hello, Zoë. How are you feeling tonight?"

"Well, thank you." Her polished English accent was polite and soft. "How come I can see you, but you aren't here?"

Good question.

"I'm in America but I wanted to check on you. So, I thought about you and now here I am."

"Oh, like magic." She smiled and it was a glorious thing.

"Yes, just like magic." I grinned.

"Is Uncle Zane with you? Can I see him too? Is he okay?" She sat up in bed and moved her head around as if she were trying to see behind me.

"He's not here right now, but we were just talking about you." That seemed to please her.

"You'll keep him safe, right?" She pointed at me.

"Yes, that's why I'm here. I won't let anyone hurt him."

"Promise?" She looked so sweet I wanted to hug her. Her concern for her uncle was earnest.

"I promise. I can tell you, he misses you terribly."

"Oh, I miss him lots and lots. I need to hug him."

And that made me think. She obviously loved him a great deal, why wouldn't she want to be with him?"

"Zoë, why didn't you want to come to America with Uncle Zane?"

She bit her lip and looked down at the bed. A secret. I could probe her mind, but I wanted her to tell me on her own.

She fidgeted just a bit.

"I promise, whatever it is, you can tell me. I'm here to protect you and keep you safe. Even though it might seem like I'm far away."

"Can you do magic to keep the bad lady away?" She looked up at me. Her big doe eyes were saucers of hope.

"What bad lady, honey?" I thought maybe someone at school might be bothering her.

"She says she's my friend, but she's kind of scary. She comes in my dreams. I don't know why, but I think she's the one who hurt my mum and dad. She feels like a monster when she comes in my dreams, but she's nice to me."

I wasn't sure what to say. The child obviously had magical abilities, which would grow to be quite powerful when she was older. It was an amazing feat that she could talk to me as she did now. And she didn't have a clue about her talent.

"Zoë, I know it's kind of scary, but can you think about the lady and show me what she looks like?"

The little girl closed her eyes. And tried to recall a dream. It's hard for any of us, especially a child who is frightened of what she sees. I saw an outline and blond hair. And I got a feeling from the presence. She didn't mean the child harm, but I could see why it would make Zoë uncomfortable. But who would do something like visit a child's dream? Well, besides me. And that was to settle Zane's mind.

When she frowned, I told her to stop thinking about the lady. I didn't want to cause the poor thing any more trauma than she'd already experienced.

"Yes, I can keep the bad lady from coming into your dreams. I'm going to send you a very pretty necklace tomorrow and I want you to never take it off. It will keep anything bad away from you. And if anyone scary does come close, it flashes a big light that will make them go away.

"For tonight, I'll say some words that will help you sleep without any fear of bad guys."

She snuggled down onto her pillow and yawned.

I realized she hadn't answered my original question.

"Zoë, why do you want to stay at school?"

She yawned big this time and stretched. Grabbing her stuffed elephant, she opened her eyes again. "If I'm here, the bad lady stays here. Then she can't get my uncle."

"You sleep tight, and I promise to check in with you every day. If you get scared, you say my name. And just like tonight I'll be there."

"Okay." She closed her eyes.

I whispered a chant and offered her protection. The poor baby thought she was protecting her uncle from the monster.

I hate monsters that prey on children. I'd find this one and destroy it. Zoë would live happily ever after, if I had anything to say about it.

Seventeen

Monday, 8 A.M.
Beverly Hills, California
Charms: 4
Spells: 2

I sent the charms to Zoë through a special courier. When Zane came into the house last night, I told him everything.

"I want to bring her here, she shouldn't be going through all of this alone." He pounded the table with his fist. "That child thinks she's protecting me from the monsters by staying away. It's wrong."

His eyes were shiny with unshed tears. Almost made me cry. Any guy who would feel so deeply about a child is okay in my book.

"It may be safer for her there at the school, Zane, at least until we get a better target. This whole thing is a giant mess. There are warlocks, neo-Nazis, and some strange woman invading Zoë's dreams. It doesn't make any sense." I shrugged.

"Well, you may be right about her being safer away from me. But I'm calling the school and sending a team of security guards to watch over her. No one is going to harm my niece."

I touched his shoulder. "On that we both agree."

I set about doing several more protection charms for the child, the prime minister and Zane. In addition, I added a few more wards for the house. No one would get in here who wasn't a friend.

Zane wanted to go out for dinner, but I didn't think we should chance it yet. There hadn't been any attempts on him yet but there was no reason to push our luck. He sent his assistant, Georgette, who arrived yesterday afternoon, after our dinner.

He wasn't in the best of moods, and to be honest who could blame him? Still haven't heard from Simone. If she doesn't show up this afternoon, I'll give her a call.

We missed our appointments for hair and eyebrows. Evidently, it's taking her longer to find the nest than she anticipated. If I hadn't been needed here, I might have gone with her. I could use some hard witch action.

I've tried several times to focus Zoë's image of the scary lady. I'm not getting anything, but I won't stop trying.

Monday, 2 P.M.

Men are so stupid. I hate them. All of them. Stupid men. Stupid, stupid, stupid.

It's been more than a week so I thought I'd try to call Sam, since I haven't heard from him. You know, just sort of wanted to make sure he was alive and well. Nothing major. I've tried to search for him mentally, but he has me blocked, the jerk.

So, I called his cell.

A woman answered.

When I asked for Sam she laughed and hung up on me.

Bitch.

Why is a woman answering Sam's phone?

Was he there? Were they laughing at me?

He wouldn't cheat on me. I know Sam. He's got trust issues out the wazoo. It's something he wouldn't even contemplate. Right?

I tried calling Azir's office, but Maridad, his assistant, said he's unavailable. I asked if he was on one of his missions, but there was silence.

"All I can tell you is that he's unavailable," she said finally. I like her a lot, and I think she has a thing for Azir, but I needed answers. She'd come to Sweet a few months ago with the sheik, and we made a connection.

"Maridad, look. I just need to get in touch with Sam. I'm pretty sure he's with Azir somewhere. I saw Azir's number on his cell. I really, really need to talk to Sam. It's an emergency."

She sighed. "I am sorry. Please understand that when these things happen, I'm not informed of the sheik's itinerary. Security reasons, I'm told." The last was said with the tiniest bit of attitude, which meant she was no happier about the situation than I was.

I took that to mean that, yes, they were on a mission. But she didn't know where they were either. Great. My supposed boyfriend and an almost boyfriend were out saving the world and doing God knows what with God knows who. Wonderful. Marvelous.

"I'm sorry if I caused you any trouble."

"Don't worry about it, and if I do hear something I'll let you know."

I think I'm going to put on a bathing suit and get some of this famous California sunshine. I'm feeling dangerous enough to even try the black two-piece. It has little shorty bottoms, and a top that covers the necessary parts (barely). No one is around today, so who cares?

8 P.M.

Sunburned witches: 1

Um, ouch. I haven't been in the sun much this summer. And well, I don't tan that well, anyway. So the fact that I fell asleep for three hours in that lovely California sun was kind of dumb on my part.

I hadn't meant to fall asleep, it just happened. I was floating in the pool trying to concentrate on anything that didn't have to do with Sam.

It didn't work well. I'm giving him the benefit of the doubt. Maybe he'd loaned the phone to someone. Or shared it. I don't know.

So I'm thinking about him and the next thing I know I'm almost drowning and Zane's pulling me up out of the water. His crazy paisley shirt and leather pants dripping, he drags me to the steps of the pool.

"Are you okay?" He pushed my hair out of my face, which felt really tight.

"Yes. I must have fallen asleep and then slipped off the raft." I walked up the steps and grabbed a towel. I handed it to him. His pants were a disaster. "I'm really sorry about your clothes. I would have been okay. When I hit the water I woke up."

He stared at me funny. "Don't worry about the clothes. You

fell just as I was rounding the corner, and I thought you might drown. How long have you been out here?"

"I don't know, what time is it?"

He looked at his watch, which must have been waterproof. If it was one of the ones he picked the day we shopped, it was worth about fifty thousand dollars, so it should be protected from hell itself.

"Bronwyn, it's six o'clock."

About three hours. I looked down at my arms. They were glowing red. Not a good sign. I turned, wrapped the towel around me, and heard Zane snicker.

"What?" I faced him again.

"Well, if I were you I'd sleep on my back tonight."

Uh?

I turned and looked at my backside in the reflection of the French doors going into the kitchen. I was paper white on one side, and Mustang red on the other. Lovely.

Zane stopped laughing when he caught my eyes.

"You know what you need is some of my very special lemonade. Run upstairs and put something comfy on, and I'll mix you a batch." He ushered me through the door.

I took a shower and put on a lotion with lots of aloe. I'm not sure but I think we might be able to cook dinner on my thighs. They are so hot, I can't stand to touch them.

I just found my big Mickey Mouse T-shirt. Now if I can find something for the bottom half we'll be in good shape.

For the hell of it, I tried to call Sam again, at home this time. No answer. I left him a message.

"Call me." That's all I said.

I'm kind of proud of myself. "You stupid fucking bastard,"

didn't come out of my mouth and I really wanted to say it. Asshole . . . Stop, Bronwyn. Breathe.

I tend to focus on the negative when it comes to relationships and think the worst. But what the hell am I supposed to think when some woman is answering his phone?

Downstairs I go for refreshments and food. I think it's time for some steak and maybe chocolate. Not necessarily in that order.

Eighteen

Beverly Hills, California

Potions: 3

Hungover witches with angry boyfriends: 1

So here's what I remember from last night: That harmless "special lemonade" was a combination of triple sec, Grand Marnier and Jack Daniel's. Unfortunately, I drank at least a pitcher before I bothered to ask what was in it.

Zane had Jacques, his favorite L.A. chef, come in and fix us steaks with about six different side dishes. There were potatoes, green beans, mushrooms, hominy and more. I can't remember everything, but I tasted it all.

Determined to eat away my troubles, I feasted like there wasn't going to be an extra ten pounds on me tomorrow.

When I asked the chef for a second steak, Zane made the mistake of saying, "Is anything wrong?"

The tears flowed. I'm sure it was the combination of sunburn, liquor and the fact that I almost died a few weeks ago.

He closed the door between the kitchen and dining room. Moving his chair next to mine, he took my hands.

"Whatever it is, love, tell me. Maybe I can help."

I sniffled. "You can't help. You're one of them."

"One of who?"

"Stupid men." I sobbed. It's so embarrassing in hindsight, but I couldn't stop crying.

He hugged me. "Yes, we can be. Does this have something to do with your doctor?"

"Stop being understanding." I pushed at his shoulder. "You're a big famous rock star. You love 'em and leave 'em. I bet you have twenty women in every town in the world who want to sleep with you. Hell, you've got millions. That's what I need to do. Just love 'em and leave 'em."

"So, what did the doctor do?" He ignored my rants.

"He just left and went to save the world and some girl answered his phone. She laughed at me."

"Who laughed at you?" Zane looked at me like I was a child.

"The woman who answered Sam's phone." I was incredulous. How could he not understand?

"So a strange woman answered your boyfriend's phone and that's sent you off the edge?" He had a knowing look in his eyes. About damn time.

Using a napkin, he dabbed the end of my nose. I'm sure I looked most attractive with snot running down my sunburned face.

"Yes." I pouted.

Then I started crying again. Big heaving sobs. He pulled me

against him, careful not to touch my sunburn. He patted my back, which was fire free. And whispered soothing words.

That's when I noticed his mouth. Zane's lips are so perfect. Not too big or small, and they are shaped like an M. He'd kissed me one day when he'd been excited, but it was just a peck. I wondered what it would be like to kiss him with more passion.

When I looked up to his face, I could see he was thinking about kissing me too.

I don't know how, but I pushed away. The motion seemed to draw him to attention. "Sorry, love. You just looked so sweet there staring up at me."

"It's okay. Zane?"

"Yes?"

I stared at him. "Right now, more than anything, I need a friend."

He smiled and took my hand. "You've got it, love. You've saved my life so many times I've stopped counting. I'll be whatever you want. What's say we get you that other steak?"

I nodded.

That's when Simone came in.

"What the fuck happened? Zane, did you make her cry?" she yelled at him.

He held up his hands. "No."

I started laughing. She's a tough one, but you gotta love Simone. She's always there for her friends.

She stared at me. "What happened? Someone answer me or I'm gonna kick both your asses."

That made me laugh harder.

Zane obviously valued his ass more than I do mine. He told her what happened with Sam.

"Bronwyn, you know he loves you. He wouldn't do anything to hurt you." Simone was serious.

She should know. When I was off with Azir a few months ago, she'd come to Sweet to recuperate from a nasty demon attack. Sam had taken care of her for me, and she tried to get in his pants. He didn't take what she offered. Thank God. She told me all about it, but before I could kill her, she said she'd done it for me. She couldn't believe there was a guy who could resist her charms. But Sam was one of them. If his love was that strong, she figured we should go full throttle toward happily ever after.

Just one problem. I don't think happily ever after is in my deck of playing cards.

I knew he loved me, or he had. "I know that, I do." And I did. "But a woman answered his phone, there's no getting around it."

She was about to say something but stopped. "Well, it's been my experience that most men are scum." She waved a hand and pointed at Zane. "Present company excluded. So, are we drowning our sorrows in booze and food? Because I could use both."

As buzzed as I felt, I realized something must have happened. Simone does a lot of wild and crazy things, but drinking isn't one of them. She must have cleaned up after the fight, because she smelled like cinnamon. She was dressed in denim shorts and a cutesy white T-shirt. Very un-Simone. She's usually dressed head to toe in leather, or low, tight jeans.

Zane went to tell the chef to throw some more steaks on the grill.

"Did you find the demons?"

She put her head in her hands, and stared at the table. "Yes."

I walked around and touched her shoulder. She's not real big on touching. When she didn't flinch, I squeezed her shoulder.

"Tell me," I whispered.

"I tracked them to a house in the mountains. They'd been taking victims there for a couple of weeks. The blood trails were strong. I had no idea how many of them were there. But when I busted in . . ."

She sighed. "Sometimes this job . . . I never know what I'm going to find."

"You don't have to talk, but I'm here."

She looked up at me. "I actually want to, but I don't want to give you the same visuals. It's too much."

So much pain in those green eyes.

"Tell me, Simone. I can take it."

She shook her head. "You probably are one of the few who could." She paused. "They were feeding on pregnant women." Turning her head, she pounded the table. She stood. Paced back and forth.

"I won't tell you exactly what I saw, but I saved the baby. I couldn't save the mother." Her voice was hushed. Hurt rode there, harsh and abrasive.

"The father was at the hospital. I couldn't face him. I gave the baby to the medical staff and told them what happened. The spook squad informed the families. I watched the husband fall to his knees. I heard his cries. I didn't get there in time to save his wife."

I saw Zane at the door. His eyes were glassy, and I knew he held tears back. So did I. Simone needed us to be strong.

I suddenly felt way too sober for the conversation. "Simone, you saved the baby and countless other lives by destroying the hive. You have to focus on the good."

Simone shook her head. "Bron, I've seen so much shit, but what they did to those women . . ."

There would be no soothing her. I whispered a small spell to give her some peace. Not to take anything way, just to help her deal with the trauma.

Zane walked in with the steaks and put them on the table, followed by the chef who held a huge cake. Pouring Simone a glass of "lemonade," Zane waited while she took a long drink. When she smiled, he refilled the glass.

The cake tasted like the inside of Oreos mixed with chocolate pudding. The frosting was like a stiff mousse. Yummers.

We were bloated, drunk and decided we needed to exercise.

But instead of the gym, Zane took us to the home theater.

It was huge. With big leather recliners, a projector screen and a stage. He turned on a karaoke machine and video camera. We sang "I Will Survive," and made our own music video.

Then we took turns doing solo performances. I warbled through Patsy Cline's "Walkin' After Midnight." Simone chose "Hey Jude." And Zane cracked us up with a rendition of Eminem's old song "Mockingbird."

Zane the rock star as a rapper. He was hilarious, and actually, pretty damn good. If this day job doesn't work out, he might do well in Detroit. Though he'd have to dog it down a bit, and throw away the Versace.

I laughed so much my stomach actually hurts today.

The next thing I knew it was morning and my cell phone was ringing. I couldn't open my eyes, but reached around trying to find the phone.

Zane answered it. "Hello? Who? Oh, yes, yes. Just a moment."

He handed me the phone. I squinted and noticed we were in my bed. Fully clothed. Simone was hanging off the other side.

"This is Bronwyn." I tried to sound businessy, even though

there was a woodpecker stabbing his beak into the middle of my forehead.

"Who was that?" Sam's question made me sit up in the bed. Grabbing my head with the pain.

"What?" I needed a moment.

"The man who answered your phone, Bronwyn. Who was he?"

"Oohh. Zane. Where are you?" I needed to change the subject. As dull as my brain was, I knew that was necessary.

"I'm home." He sounded sullen.

"You sound tired. Is everything okay?"

Then I remembered about the woman who answered his phone. I was supposed to be angry with him.

"I called to tell you I was back. Obviously you're busy."

It took me a minute. "No, no. I was asleep. Oh, no, it isn't what you think. We just passed out. Simone and Zane . . . We all had a bit too much to drink last night and . . . well to be honest I'm not sure how we ended up here, but nothing happened." I rattled on.

"Bronwyn, I can't deal with this right now." He was angry.

"Wait a minute. Before you go off on one of your I-can't-trust-the-world speeches, I'll have you know that I called your phone yesterday and a woman answered. So tell me, Sam. Who answered *your* phone?"

He grunted. "I don't know."

"That's not an answer, Sam. You can think the worst of me, I'm trying not to do that with you." Well I was, but hell.

"I don't know because my phone was stolen while we were in the jungle. I was going to give you my new number but right now I see very little use in it."

He hung up.

Argh!

Stupid men. Stolen phone. Argh!

Why were his stories always so much better than mine? It wasn't fair.

I've got to mix some more hangover potions for all of us. Then, when my brain stops beating against my skull, I'll try calling him gain.

So, I was in bed with Zane and Simone. It wasn't like anything happened. Of course he didn't know that, but still.

Oh, crap.

Nineteen

Wednesday, 4 P.M.
Beverly Hills, California
Charms: 3
Spells: 3
Witches with new Marc Jacobs sparkly Mary Janes: 1

I couldn't stop him. Trust me, I tried.

Zane proclaimed today National Shopping Till We Drop Day. Cabin fever had infected his mind and he had to get out of the house.

With Simone and me in tow, we hit Rodeo Drive first. I saw it some in London, but we are even more celebrity crazed here. For most of the day we were able to hold the general public away from Zane, but that didn't keep the salespeople from falling all over themselves to please him.

We began the day, as all good shoppers should, at the Giorgio

Armani Boutique. My mom's the shopaholic of our family, but I do have penchant for clean lines, fantastic shoes and anything that makes my butt look good.

After Armani, we made stops at Prada, Chanel, Louis Vuitton and Hugo Boss. Simone, who lives in leather pants (harder for demon claws to get through) and minuscule tops, actually got into the fun.

I think maybe she needed something to take her mind off of the demon battle yesterday.

In Prada, Zane insisted we try on these awesome shoes.

"If you ever tell anyone how much I'm enjoying this, I'll slit your throat," Simone whispered while we paraded in front of the mirrors looking at our fabulous legs in Prada heels.

"Hey, that goes two ways, girlfriend. Have you ever in your life seen a straight man who loved shopping so much?" I tried on a pair of sassy light blue pumps with a tiny strap around the ankle.

She laughed. "No. Did you see how much money he spent at Armani? My God, if he didn't raise so much for starving children, I'd have a serious problem with the guy."

Checked myself in the mirror. My sunburn had faded to a light honey color and no longer hurt. "That's what makes him so interesting. I'm not the best psychoanalyst, but I think he uses shopping as a way of taking control. Like if he can buy things and have whatever he wants, then the world is a better place. I don't know." I pulled on a pair of yellow sandals. "I need a pedicure."

Simone thumped herself on the head. "Oh shit, I'm so sorry. I forgot all about our beauty day."

I put a hand on her arm. "Hey, you were busy saving the world. Besides, we can do it some other time."

"I'll call the great almighty stylist. God, David will be so pissed. It takes forever to get in. But he loves and adores me, and I think he might even be a little afraid of me. I'll get us another appointment."

She pulled out her cell and walked around the corner.

Zane came back and he and his assistant were loaded down with bags. Two of the security guards from Zane's entourage hauled everything out to the car.

"So, luv, fancy anything from my beloved Prada?" He was dressed in jeans today. They were faded, striped, ragged on the end and probably cost five hundred bucks. His white shirt had sheer stripes through it, and his sunglasses were balanced on his head.

"Not today. It looks like you didn't have any trouble." I pointed to the bags as they went out on the bulky shoulders of the guards.

"All in a day's work, love, all in day's work." He grabbed a champagne flute from the silver tray on the table beside a shoe display.

Zane frowned and I wondered what could be bothering him. "For a man who has been in his element the last three hours, you don't look happy."

"Maybe it's from all the drinking the other night, but I feel strange." He touched a hand to his head.

I moved to him and felt his forehead. I don't know why people check for a fever first when someone doesn't feel well, but it's automatic. His temperature was normal.

I pushed him into the chair, and looked him over. Sent my mind through his body looking for any kind of illness. All his vital organs were strong and there was no trace of anything unusual.

Simone walked in. "Hey, what's wrong? Why are you doing mojo on Zane?" She turned to survey the store. "Did I miss something?"

Zane shook his head. "All I said was that I felt strange, and the witch shoved me in a chair. I think she's X-raying me or something."

I shushed them both, as I did a final read. Nothing.

"I don't see anything." I opened my eyes to find them both staring.

"I told you I only felt strange, not bad—weird. Maybe anxious is a better word." Zane threw up his hands.

"Should we go home?" Simone took his pulse, I think more to annoy him than anything. "Maybe you're worried about the concert."

He rolled his eyes. "I think we need a change of venue. Let's head to Melrose and see what we can find."

Back in the limo, I continued to watch him. I noticed a sign of anxiousness, if he was at all precognitive and most people are, it meant trouble was on the way.

We hit Fred Segal, Alan K and the vintage shop Wasteland. It was outside of the sexy lingerie store Agent Provocateur, don't ask why we were there, that I noticed a tinge of magic.

Simone sensed something too. We both cased the store, and as she went one way, I went the other. I did a quick mind sweep but didn't see anything. But when I stepped outside, a pile of black sludge came swinging toward me. I moved and volleyed it back to the perpetrator.

He was dressed in a black cloak, not at all appropriate for the eighty-degree weather we were enjoying.

"Show yourself, warlock." I used the voice. My mother has

the same one. When I was a kid she'd yell, "Bronwyn," in that voice and it made me cry. Didn't work on the warlock.

"Die, witch." His voice reverberated, the same kind of trick I'd used. Why couldn't just one of these guys come up with something more original than "Die, witch"?

He turned and lobbed another ball of ick toward me. God, were we going to play this game all day?

I sent my mind to his and tried to read it. His brain shut down like a metal door on steroids. Fine. This was something new for me, usually I just burn the bad guys from the inside out, and asked questions later.

Starting with his feet, I sent heat, but he was unaffected.

Chanting, he raised his arms above his head, then he disappeared.

"Behind you." Simone yelled. Some time during the battle she'd moved to the other side of the street, waiting I'm sure for the right moment to strike.

I turned just in time to miss his attack.

When she yelled, he threw sludge at her and she ducked and rolled out of the way. He threw another ball and it missed her by inches.

As much as I needed information from this idiot, I wasn't about to let him hurt her. The sludge wouldn't kill her, but it might incapacitate her for a few days.

I couldn't use my new power of shaking the earth to knock him down. It was too unstable, but I could throw fire at him.

With my mind, I built the energy from my solar plexus into small fireballs, one for each hand. I tossed one and then another. He dodged them both and began his chant again.

The thing is, he wasn't that powerful and it made me angry

that he could move through space the way he did. That's something I've wanted to do for a very long time. But, no. I can shake the earth. Woo hoo.

I stomped my foot in a childish fit of envy, and the asphalt road shook. Oops. I hadn't meant to do that. The warlock fell down and I threw another ball of fire at him. It caught his pants leg and he moved around violently. Before he could make it to his knees I threw another. That's when I saw his eyes. They weren't just orange contacts. They were fiery demon eyes from hell.

"My master will kill you, witch," he screamed just before he became a pile of ash.

I felt them before I heard the sirens. The spook squad arrived with a paddy wagon. Unfortunately, there was nothing to paddy. Brooms would have been more helpful.

"She didn't leave much." Simone's so good with the obvious.

"Inspector Cole said to expect this." One of the officers squatted to get a closer look at the ashes.

"Is he here?" I looked past him at the three others. I didn't see Cole's blond hair among them.

"No, ma'am, he's flying in from New York. He just radioed and said to tell you he'll be stopping by this evening."

Well if Cole wanted to be involved, that was good. He's a much better detective than me. Though I out-magic him about a hundred to one. I hadn't seen him since he saved my life a few months ago, but we had e-mailed. I also knew he was involved in Garnout's coven troubles in New York.

"Is that the Cole, who helped you kill Blackstock?" Simone looked down the street and then motioned the limo to come around the corner.

"Yes, I think you met him at the hospital, but it was so crazy I can't remember."

She shrugged as if it didn't matter to her one way or another. Then she ushered Zane into the car.

"Well, if you guys can take care of this," I pointed to the dust, "I'll be going."

"Yes, ma'am. As I said, Inspector Cole will be by later."

"Thanks." When I first met Cole I hadn't trusted him, but that had changed when he laid his hand on me and healed me enough to destroy our mutual enemy Blackstock.

In the limo, Zane and Georgette were going back and forth. "Can you believe she did it again? She saved my life. We're three for three."

I smiled and tuned them out.

Simone shook her head and I nodded.

The black sludge and "Die, witch" meant something.

We both knew that warlock hadn't been after Zane, he'd been waiting for me.

Twenty

Witches following the whims of a crazy rock star: 1

When Monsieur Zane wants a change of venue, he means it. After the mini-battle on Melrose we went back to the house in Beverly Hills. We walked in and Zane announced, "We're moving, my loves. I can't stand this place a moment longer. We need the beach and a clean ocean breeze."

I didn't have the heart to mention that there wasn't any clean air left in the greater Los Angeles area.

He turned to Georgette. "Tell them to get the house ready in Malibu, doll. Make sure we have extra security for the beach."

She raised a pierced eyebrow, but flipped on her cell phone and went to work. Her clipped British tone barked orders.

Whirling in a circle, Zane clapped his hands. "Let's pack it up."

Then he left with a flourish. Simone shrugged and I did the same.

I love the beach.

In less than an hour we were out the door. It's amazing what you can do when you have unlimited funds.

So now we are happily ensconced in a beachfront property that must cost at least a zillion dollars. The house is bigger than his castle in England. It sits up in a cliff and there's a steep path down to a private beach.

Everything is white, off-white and pale blue. Very serene.

It's much cooler here and feels more like the September weather one would expect in California.

We had dinner out on one of the huge decks. There's an end-less pool on that one that makes it look like you could swim right off the edge and over the cliff. I'm not afraid of heights, but did feel a bit of vertigo when I reached the edge.

Cole showed up midway through dinner and Zane invited him to join us. Here's the thing about Cole. I like him, but I al-ways feel like he's looking beyond. He's listening to what you say, but at the same time he's getting more out of it than you might mean.

That cop instinct is so strong in him. I watched as he talked with Zane tonight. Interesting.

We were at a large Moroccan-tiled table loaded down with everything from crab to lobster and shrimp. Absolutely one of my favorite meals since I've been here.

The ocean breeze had turned chilly and I pulled my sweater over my arms.

"So how does one become one of the leading officers of the International Magical Inspectors?" Zane's question surprised me because I was equally curious about the answer.

Simone sat on Cole's left, but she didn't seem very interested. She kept looking out at the horizon, as if she was waiting for something.

Cole leaned forward, elbows on the table. His expression turned serious. "Well, let's see. My mother was a witch, my father a warlock. He worked as an inspector, as did my grandfather."

Zane nodded. "So you had little choice?"

"Oh, I had a choice. In fact I was in college studying biophysics and had planned to work in the sciences."

Simone turned back and stared at him. She is a biophysicist and also has a Ph.D. in statistics. Of course, she prefers slaying demons for a living, but her education gives her a one-up like nobody's business.

Cole, who was dressed casual in jeans and light green shirt, continued. "I knew so much about magic, but I wanted to learn why we, being magical folks, are different from ordinary humans. I had my future all planned out."

He frowned. "Making a long story short, I got a call that my father had been killed in the line of duty. I applied for my inspector's license that day. Went home for the funeral and then began my criminology studies. Been in the field almost ten years now."

Leaning back in the chair, he faced me.

"We have a real problem with this one." His sudden change of subject threw me.

"You mean the warlocks?" I scooted my chair so I could see him better in the waning light.

"The whole thing. It's all connected. The warlocks in New York, London, here. And the demon. Even Simone's nest. They're related."

Simone held up a hand. "That wasn't mine, I destroyed it, but those evil bastards had nothing to do with me."

He touched her shoulder and she stared at him. An evil Simone stare. She's not usually like that with men. Honestly, Simone will jump in bed with anything male. Well, human male, no demons. She's a huge flirt and men fall over themselves to touch her.

I'd never seen a man as disinterested in her as Cole, and she detested him too, I could tell. But why? They'd met months ago when Blackstock attacked, but I'd never heard her say anything about him.

"Didn't mean to offend, Simone," he said. "You know what I meant."

She shrugged. "Whatever."

He shifted his attention back to me. "The warlocks and wannabes are a part of a cult. They're all over the world. They worship the demon Blaseus. Not a lot is known about him, except that he has great power and uses his minions to do his bidding, while he plays it safe in hell.

"We've got some dimension jumpers doing research, but so far we haven't had a lot of luck."

I bit my lip. Didn't want to bring it up in front of everyone but I wanted to know if he knew why the warlocks and demons had been after both Zane and me.

"So, why would they come after one of the world's leading rock stars? Usually Blaseus types don't call attention to themselves until they're ready to take over the world." I played with the crystal salt and pepper shakers. The atmosphere at the beach house was casual, but the table setting was something you'd see at the Ritz. A low flower arrangement sat in the middle surrounded by crystal and pale vanilla china.

"That's what's strange—" Cole stopped when Simone suddenly turned in her chair.

Her eyes cut to him. "It isn't Blaseus; someone's using him." She frowned. "I'd put money on it. Think about it. That strong of a demon is too smart to pull these stupid stunts against a witch like Bronwyn. And he wouldn't advertise his demon minions. So he's made a deal with someone."

I could see the wheels click in Cole's head. "Yes, but who?"

Simone turned away again to stare at the water. The waves were huge as they crashed against the rocks and the sound was louder than it had been when we came out. "I don't have a clue," she whispered.

Zane had been quiet through all this. "Do you know why they're after me?" He had no expression on his face. He wanted an answer so bad I could feel it, but he wouldn't let Cole know that.

Cole sighed. "I'm sorry, no. Until we find out what's behind all of this, it's impossible to know. But I do know that you aren't the only one singled out."

He faced me and I knew what he meant. He'd known the same as Simone and me that I'd become a target at some point. That didn't narrow the field of bad guys. Just about anyone on the side of evil wanted me dead. If they didn't, I hadn't met them yet.

"Well, Cole, you're a cheery one." Zane laughed. "I don't

know about you, but I could use a cup of tea. Too much doom and gloom. Why don't we move our little gathering inside?"

"I should be going." Cole stood. "I've got to look over the evidence from this afternoon."

Simone snorted. "There's nothing left."

Cole smiled. "There usually isn't after Bronwyn gets done with them, but there's enough for us to start tracing."

"Bron." Simone grabbed her bags from our shopping excursion. "I'm heading out. I want to run by the lab. You can catch me on the cell if you need me." She paused mid-step and looked out the windows. The view of the ocean was visible from the entire back of the house.

"Not telling you how to do your job, but put some more wards on the back of the house. Something's out there. I can feel it, but it isn't ready to attack yet."

I never like to delve into Simone's life too far. She doesn't like it, but I had to know. "Wait, what's your deal with Cole?"

Frowning she shook her head. "He saved your life."

"And that's a bad thing?"

"No, idiot, it makes me feel like I owe him something. And I don't like debts of any kind with men."

She turned and walked out the door.

Well, okay.

I'd sensed the same thing she did about the evil, but in a different way. I didn't think it was actually out in the ocean. It was just out there, in the universe somewhere.

After Cole left, I wanted to console Zane, but I didn't know how. He was much more upset than he let on outside. I knew exactly how he felt. When Blackstock had come after me, I didn't even know the warlock had existed. I always have hits on me, but usually it's because I've killed someone they love, or I've thrown a wrench in their dastardly plans to take over the world.

I found Zane in the kitchen. He leaned back against the counter and shook his head. "I don't get it. I always thought the world of magic sounded so exotic. I was jealous that my family seemed sadly lacking. Now I wish I could get as far away from it as possible."

I laughed, but it wasn't a happy sound. "There are times when I wish I could escape it too." I touched his hand and he grabbed hold of mine.

I had a sudden inspiration. "Here, hold on tight, I know something that will make you smile." I zoned in on little Zoë. Said a small chant and opened my eyes.

"Look into my eyes, Zane. This is the good part of magic."

He pulled a little on my hand as if he wanted to get away.

"No, Zane, look."

He must have seen Zoë. "Oh, it's my girl. Look at her, sleeping so peacefully."

I tried not to blink so that he could see her clearly.

Sighing, he squeezed my hand. I closed my eyes.

"Thank you, Bronwyn. I needed to see her. She's safe isn't she?"

"Yes, she's well protected." I moved to the back of the house. "Come on, you can watch me put out the wards. If you're really nice, I'll make you a new amulet for protection. A gorgeous one that matches Zoë's. That way, if either one of you finds yourself in danger your amulets will both glow."

He shook his head and laughed. "I'm glad I have you as my guardian witch, luv."

"Damn right you are."

I threw my hands up and created a small ball of fire in the center of the room. Began the chant to place the wards.

Door to door
Window to window
With this flame I protect all within
Evil shall not pass these borders.
As I will, so mote it be.

The energy spun away from me. It was something you could more feel than see.

"Wow, I'm back to thinking magic is cool." Zane's eyes were huge.

I smiled and patted him on the back.

"Let's go make you a pretty new doodad for your neck."

Thursday, 2 A.M.

I want to call Sam so bad right now. I woke up in the middle of a dream about him. It wasn't one of those where we shared the excitement.

The dream was about his hands. How he plays my body with perfection every time he touches me. Could feel his hand sliding up my thigh, teasing between my legs and then plunging inside me. Then his lips on me.

God, I woke up in a sweat, needy and body aching.

I need Sam. Dammit. I need him.

This sucks.

I'm going to call him in the morning. I don't care how mad he is at me. I will work this out.

Thursday, 10 A.M.

Malibu, California

Soon to be sassily beautiful witches: 1

Simone just called. Evidently she'd been on patrol last night. She sounded exhausted. I asked her if she'd been after something specific.

"No, not really. Had an idea about something, but it didn't go the way I expected." She yawned.

Of course I yawned right after she did. They are contagious, especially when you've had only three hours of sleep.

"I called to let you know that we have appointments with Sir David at two. We're doing the works this afternoon. I'll pick you up around one. The traffic can be shit coming in from Malibu."

"That sounds like fun, Simone, but I can't leave Zane behind."

"I'm not asking you to. He's the reason David's forgiven me so quickly for missing our last appointment. He can't wait to get his hands on Zane's hair."

"Zane has highlights?"

"Bronwyn, sometimes you are so naive. Do you think blond hair looks like that naturally? This should be a hoot. I can't wait to see what he does for you. Don't forget to be ready at one."

She hung up. I decided to get a couple of hours of sleep. I thought about maybe doing it out by the pool, but it would take too much effort to move.

I'll just snuggle down here, and dream about the beautiful new 'do Sir David will bestow upon me.

Twenty-one

Witches hanging with the famous people: I

I'm so fucking gorgeous. I can't believe it. Simone was right about Sir David, he is the master with hair. We're still here. I have my glass of champagne, my journal and I'm sitting in this massive massage chair while Sasha finishes my pedicure.

The whole place is very modern. White couches, chocolate walls and candles everywhere.

David's doing Simone's auburn highlights now. Of course they aren't called auburn, they're like hot mocha red fudge or something.

Me, I'm chai tea mixed with mango and my hair actually glows.

Zane's in the middle of a facial with Lilly. She's already sucked all the nastiness from my skin. It glows too. I feel like a new woman.

David coerced my waves into spiral curls that fall all over my head. I love it. Have no idea how he did it, or if I could ever replicate it, but I'm loving it right now.

David shut down the salon for Zane. The power of celebrity in Los Angeles. I swear. But it's okay because I happened to realize today that I don't mind the star treatment at all. We're his only clients for this afternoon.

Cool. It's time for my makeup application with Tara. I can't wait.

Thursday, 6 P.M.

Well, up until five minutes ago we were three incredibly beautiful people with nowhere to go. It isn't safe to do much in public, but Zane has a friend at a club who wants us to come to the back room.

"We can eat, dance, whatever we want," Zane said. "And watch everyone below. No one will even know we're there."

I wasn't sure. I didn't the like the idea of us being anywhere innocents could be caught in the crossfire.

"Come on, Bron, a little dancing will do us good." Simone laughed. Her mood had lightened since we left Sir David's. Possibly because he'd given her a sleek head of hair that was so shiny I swear I could see myself in it.

They both stared at me across the seat of the limo. "Fine," I sighed. "But the first hint of trouble and we are out of there."

We've come all the way back to the Malibu house to change. Zane's need for a change of venue hasn't been the most economical in the way of time. We also have to stop at the Staples Center to see how the stage is going for his concert. There were problems with some lift at the rehearsals in London, so they want to make sure all is well.

It's funny. I sometimes forget he's one of the most famous faces in the world. As campy and silly as he can be at times, he's "just another bloke." His words, not mine.

Now, what to wear?

2 A.M.

The club was called Mac's. Doesn't sound like much, and didn't look like much from the outside. Of course we were coming in from the back.

Inside it was a different story. We walked up the back stairs to the second floor, it's on the side of the normal VIP room where most of the A-list celebrities hang out. This room was for even more special guests. Thank you, Zane.

The windows were mirrored on the other side, so no one could see us. Security stayed outside the door, and Zane, Simone and myself had a dining area and dance floor to ourselves. There was also a bank of televisions on one wall so we could see all the dancers up close.

"Oh yes, look at this one." Zane used the remote to focus in on a young woman in a yellow T-shirt and short black leather mini. She didn't wear a bra and was at least a D cup. Her breasts were bobbing to the music in a hypnotic rhythm.

"This is so wrong." I moved to the large window across the main wall. "We can watch them from here, without spying on them so close."

"Oh geez, Bron, get a grip." Simone grabbed the remote. "Now there, my friends, that's something worthy of a close-up.

She pushed the button so that the camera zoned in on a pair of jeans. I couldn't see the guy's face, but he was obviously excited by the girl next to him. His dick was hard against the fabric of his too-tight jeans and it had to be at least nine inches long.

I crossed my legs. Blowing out a breath, I grabbed Zane's hand. "Let's dance."

He laughed. "Oh baby." He gyrated his hips up and down.

"No." I pushed him about two feet away from me. "I'll dance here and you dance there."

Simone had been nibbling on the last of the sushi they'd brought up. I don't mind the tuna, shrimp and avocado rolls, but the rest—well, it made me hungry for Lulu's fried chicken. I bet if Zane ever tried Lulu's he'd get off this healthy eating kick. Of course, it would ruin him for life.

Thinking of Lulu's made me think of home. And Sam. I wondered what he was doing right now. I had dialed his number this morning, but I never pushed Send. I did take my picture with my glorious new hair and saved it on my phone. I may send it later.

Zane was doing his best to distract me and it almost worked. He and Simone had moved into a clinch and were doing some warped version of the tango. She had a daisy in her teeth, and he twirled her out and then tight against his body.

Their dancing did make me forget about Sam for a moment, but that's also when I felt a twinge of something. Simone must have noticed too. I saw her stiffen and look at the wall of televisions.

We both tried to see what we felt, but none of the faces gave me anything. I sent my mind out, and let me tell you, half-naked people in a club think some raunchy crap. I saw three-ways, four-ways and some bondage ideas. Wow, that one was interesting.

But as hard as I tried, I couldn't find whoever it was in the mass of humanity.

"Zane, we need to go. Whoever is down there probably doesn't mean us harm, but we can't chance getting caught here with so many innocent bystanders." I'd read their minds, and they weren't so innocent. But I didn't think any of them had plans to die tonight.

"What's wrong?" Zane went on alert.

"Someone's here and I can't get into their head, so it's best if we go."

Simone grabbed Zane's leather jacket from the chair and pushed him to the door. "I'm going downstairs to see if I can locate him. If he's a demon or warlock, I should be able to sense him—or her, if it's a witch."

I took one last look out the window. A dark-haired man with beautiful brown eyes looked at me from the corner by the large center bar. He smiled.

But I knew he couldn't see me. Then he disappeared.

"That's it, we're outta here." I shoved Zane to the door.

"I saw him, Simone, but he's vanished. If he can do that . . . Let's just go."

We took the back stairs and I loaded Zane in the limo. More than anything I wanted to stay and investigate, but I couldn't take the chance that this might be a trap. Many times bad warlocks have tried to lure me away from my charges. I also didn't want to chance Simone getting hurt, though I'd never tell her that.

"Simone, if they attack us in transit I'm going to need you with us."

She hesitated a moment outside the car and then jumped in.

Zane laughed, but I could see his hands shaking. "You girls certainly know how to add some excitement to a night."

I smiled at Simone. "Yep, we're just two hot chicks who know how to party."

Simone pulled out a bottle of champagne from the limo fridge and popped the cork. "That's right." She did all of this while keeping an eye on the road searching for anyone who might follow.

I wanted to hug her, but figured I'd get a punch in the gut for trying.

We made it home without incident, but the whole thing at the club made me very uneasy.

That guy wanted me to notice him. His smile had been an invitation.

To what? That's the question.

3 A.M.

Zane woke me banging on the door.

"My amulet's glowing," he screamed. It was more of a panicked scream than anything else. I checked the wards on the house with my mind, but found nothing.

Then it dawned on me. "Zoë," we both said it at the same time.

I closed my eyes and centered on the child. She sat in the middle of her bed holding Tuttles the elephant tight. "I can't remember your name, I can't remember your name." She kept saying it over and over, her eyes shut with fear.

"It's okay, Zoë, it's Bronwyn, I'm here. Open your eyes. Uncle Zane is here too."

Zane was staring into my eyes so that she could see us both.

"Zoë, look around the room. Is everything okay?" I kept my voice calm.

"It wasn't real. It felt like she was there but she wasn't. She tried to get my dream." Zoë looked at Zane. "I don't know who she is, Uncle, she says she's my friend. But she doesn't feel like it."

She saw the woman again, and she shouldn't have, because I had that child protected. The only people she could dream about were her family and friends.

"Zoë, honey. I know you were so scared, and I'm proud of you for being brave. But I need you to be quiet for just a second. Look at Uncle Zane."

She did what I asked. Her big moon eyes pleaded with his. I could feel his pulse through my hand. He was frightened for her.

I gently went through her mind, rewinding her dream slightly so I could see. The vision wasn't clear. The woman's silhouette was visible through a window. But I couldn't see her face.

Damn. I brought myself out and stared at Zane. I shook my head, so he'd know that I didn't find what I looked for.

"Zoë, who is this woman you told Bron about, have you ever seen her outside of your dreams?"

The little girl shrugged. "I don't think so. She doesn't want to be mean, but she can't help it, Uncle. She wants to be a good person."

"Luv, how do you know?" He squeezed my hand so hard it hurt. I don't think he realized it, but I didn't want to break contact with him.

"She told me a long time ago. A friend, she said she's always been my friend."

I didn't know what to tell him. The woman could be real, or she could be a character from a dream.

Saying a soothing spell, I calmed Zoë down. It was morning

there and time for her to get up, but I didn't want her starting her day afraid.

Her breathing slowed and she smiled.

"The necklace worked. I couldn't think of your name but I grabbed it and yelled for Uncle Zane in my dreams."

"How very smart of you, Poppet." He smiled back at her. "I'm so proud of you."

Her eyes lit up. "Thank you, Bronwitch."

I smiled. I'd been called lots worse. One of the boys in high school used to call me Bronbitch. I grew to like it, especially when my powers came in. At our senior party his pants just happened to slip around his ankles and everyone saw him for the pencil dick he was.

"You're welcome, Zoë."

Zane said a few more words, and then I checked on the guards. They were alert and standing just outside her door.

It's five A.M. in Sweet. I'm sending Sam the picture I took of me and my beautiful new hair, in an e-mail. Maybe my curly tresses and glowing skin will incite him into forgiving me.

I know it's a reach, but sometimes a girl's gotta pull out all the stops.

Twenty-two

Malibu, California
Backup-singing witches: 1 (Just kidding)

The concert rehearsals go into full gear today. We're headed out to an airplane hangar where Zane says they've set up a stage.

"We'll go through the show just to make sure we don't have any rough spots." Zane was downstairs early this morning. Well, ten, that's early for him. He's also changed his diet. Lean protein and fruits and vegetables.

"Hanging out with you hasn't done a thing for my figure." He pointed to his incredibly slim waist. There wasn't a speck of fat on his body. I'd seen him by the pool. He was slim but had a stomach most men would kill for, and his upper arm strength was evident.

I'd never tell him any of that. His ego had enough inflation. But if he thought eating healthy helped his performance, who am I to argue?

"That's fine, as long as you don't make me eat all that healthy crap." I pointed to the bowl of fruit, which actually looked really good. There was kiwi in there. Man, I love kiwi. Didn't dare eat it in front of Mr. Healthy, though.

"I'm going for a swim in the pool. Want to join me?" He walked toward the kitchen.

"Exercise and dieting. Forget it. I'm going to scrounge up some pancakes and take a nap."

That made him laugh.

Actually, I grabbed some kiwi, and came back upstairs to get charms ready. I also had to figure out a way to protect Zane, the band and the twenty thousand people at the Staples Center a week from now. I'm powerful, but that stretches even my limits.

I e-mailed Garnout and asked if he had any ideas. And checked my phone about a dozen times to see if Sam called. If he could resist my picture I sent him last night, well, I refuse to think about it. Maybe he hasn't checked his e-mail yet.

8 P.M.

I'm exhausted. This rock star crap is tiring. But fun. As soon as we got out to the hangar, I put wards up to keep any unwanted visitors away.

Zane was all business. I honestly thought he'd be a bit of a prima donna, but he isn't. The way he treats his band, backup singers and crew with such kindness says a lot about him.

One of his singers wasn't feeling well. I sent her a healing spell, but Zane insisted she rest.

That's when the fun began.

"Bronwyn, can you help us out?" He motioned me up on the stage.

If he hadn't said my name, I would have pretended not to notice him. I climbed up the stairs in the back.

I walked up to him. "You rang, master?"

"Cute. Here, stand in between Chris and Jenny so we can get this blocked. Follow along with them. They'll show you what to do."

I held up a hand. "Wait a minute, I'm not a singer."

"Then don't sing, but stand there and move around with them so we can make sure the staging and lighting works."

"Fine." I put my hands on my hips.

Chris and Jenny were quite lovely. They showed me everything, and I'll never tell Zane, but I had the time of my life. I even hummed along to some of the tunes I knew. By the third song, I caught on to some of the hand motions and dance steps. They repeat a lot, but mix it up for each song.

Can't wait to get home and show Kira and Margie. Maybe we'll have a private karaoke night and I can teach them all I learned.

I'm worn out, though. Still not exactly going full strength yet. I wanted to practice today and use my new power, but this being California, didn't think they'd appreciate me shaking the ground on a whim.

Haven't heard from Garnout. Or Sam.

I don't understand how he can love me so much and think the

worst. As bad as it may have sounded, he had to know that I would never do anything to hurt him. Well, obviously he doesn't know that or he'd answer my calls and e-mails.

Relationships suck.

II P.M.

Had a voice mail from Garnout. He's sending some spells that will help with concert security next week. I also had an e-mail from Sam.

"Bronwyn, I can't do this right now. I'm sorry. I need some time to sort things out. Everything is such a mess.—Sam"

The thing is, I'm not really sure what exactly he's needing time for, and I know that sounds insane. Does he mean what happened with Zane? Is he still trying to get over that meeting with his ex?

Oh, the phone is ringing. Maybe it's him.

4 A.M.

I just thought I was tired before. Simone called from the road.

"I'm picking you up in ten minutes, be ready."

She pulled up on her motorcycle, and I ran out to the circular drive. I'd thrown on a pair of jeans and a blue T-shirt that says *La Merde se Produit,* which is Shit Happens in French.

"Simone, you know I can't leave the house. I've got to be here for Zane." I rubbed my arms to ward off the chill in the night air.

"I don't have time to explain. Do your hocus-pocus so no one can get in the house until we come back and grab some of your mojo kit. We're going demon hunting." Her face was a mask of calm, but her voice had an edge.

I ran back in and grabbed some charms and potions and stuck them in a small bag. Knocked on Zane's door.

He was surprised to see me. "What's up, luv?"

"I'm putting some wards on the house. Don't try to go out or let anyone in until I get back. If anyone tries to pass the wards, well, it won't be pretty."

"But—" He yelled as I ran back down the hall.

Simone pushed a helmet on my head and handed me a leather jacket. We took off down the highway.

Usually trouble finds me. Unlike Simone, I seldom go looking for it.

She reached back and pushed something on my helmet. No easy feat since we were going about one hundred and ten miles an hour.

"Bron?" Her voice came into the helmet.

"Yes?"

"Sorry, forgot to click your comm button when I put the helmet on you. Look, we're going into a nest of Arnoks."

"Arnoks?" Here? Oh, my God.

"Those acid-spitting demon assholes are going to die. I thought about going in on my own, but I'd have to kill them all. I thought if you were there maybe you could get into their heads before I destroy them."

Smart girl. Acid-spitting demons were rare. There was a chance they might be connected to the one in London.

"How did you find them?"

She cackled. "Bronwyn, I'm a demon slayer. This is what I do. But to answer the question, there's been a high incidence of missing persons and pets in this neighborhood. Something's been feeding."

Yuck.

Five minutes later we were pulling up at the end of a block of ranch houses. Except for the landscaping, every house looked the same.

"We walk from here." She pulled off her helmet.

I followed her and we walked about six houses down. I thought maybe she'd be a bit stealthier. Hiding in bushes, that sort of thing, but she didn't. She stood in front of the house.

"Damn." She marched up to the front door and kicked it open. I stood in the street not sure what to do. If something came at her, I could hit it with fire or one of the stunning potions I held in my hands.

She walked in and didn't come out. So, I decided to follow. The stench, a cross between rotting eggs and dead rats, filled my senses. It almost made me gag.

I put my sleeve in front of my face and moved inside. Except for a smashed coffee table, the living room looked exactly like what you'd expect in a home like this. Sofa, television in the corner and couple of chairs.

"Don't come in here," Simone yelled from what looked like the kitchen. "Fuck."

But I was halfway there by the time she said it and I saw them.

Piles of body parts and animal carcasses lying on the kitchen floor. The blood pooled and the smell was unbearable. I had to turn around. I said a healing spell to the spirits of the dead and kindly asked them to move toward the light of the blessed world.

I could feel their energy, confusion and anger.

So could my friend Simone.

Fury burned in her eyes.

She walked past and stopped to let me finish my chant.

"Make sure you tell them they will be avenged." She growled.

I understood. We would find these evil things. We would kill them.

And we would enjoy it.

Twenty-three

Saturday, 5 P.M.

Malibu

Spells: 1

Probably ex-boyfriends who have called: 0

After another full day of rehearsals, Zane wanted to go out again tonight, or have friends over, but I've advised against it. I see his need to be adored, but we can't risk pulling anyone else into this mess.

But he's insisted so we'll be making our way to the limo in about a half hour. Zane says they don't normally do premieres on weekends.

"This one is tied to save the whales or something, so since it's for charity they are making it an even bigger party than usual." He grabbed his chin. "That means it's time to glam it up big time."

Thank goodness I've brought my leather pants and another adorable halter top from London. This one is made out of white lacy material that looks see-through but isn't. It's really soft and comfortable.

Simone isn't happy about going. She wants to hunt the demons. So do I. But unfortunately I can't keep watch over him and help her.

My reason, and the only way I could get her to go, is to tell her Zane and I were like bait. What these morons wanted most was a rock star and witch. So what better place to go public?

Of course the fact we were putting hundreds of lives in danger to do so has crossed my mind.

Zane insists the premiere will be good for all of us.

"The security nowadays is basically one guard per celebrity, plus we all bring our own. It's probably safer than sitting here at home." He stood in his enormous closet picking something to wear. I've never seen a man with so many clothes.

I sat on his bed shaking my head in the affirmative or negative, depending on what he pulled out.

He had a point about the safety issues.

Still, I'd bring backup with my potions and spells.

He finally chose a pair of black leather pants, and a deep red poet's shirt. Thanks to his time by the pool, he'd lost his English paleness and had a healthy glow. The red would pop against his skin.

Laying the clothes on his bed, he put a hand on my shoulder.

"I know it hasn't been easy for you this last week. And I'm sorry about the troubles with your boyfriend." He sighed. "It bothers me how much I've come to depend on you for my security."

I patted the hand on my shoulder. "Yep, I've kind of grown attached to you too. But we've got to get this settled soon, and not because of my man troubles. People are dying and we've got to stop it."

"I'm worried about the concert. It's only a few days away and if—I couldn't take it."

I stood up. "I know, me either. We'll take care of it, don't worry." Just to be mean, and to get his mind off his troubles I pointed at his hair. "Hey, is that a gray hair?"

His eyes were wide with shock, and his hand flew to his head. "What? No!" He ran to his bathroom.

I laughed all the way down the hall. It was cruel, but it did get his mind off the evil haunting us.

Now I've got to get ready. I hope I can get in those pants. I've eaten an awful lot the last couple of days.

11:30 P.M.
This has to be one of the worst nights of my life. Okay, maybe not the worst, but certainly right up there in the top ten.

At least we all looked good.

Simone showed up in her black leather bustier and matching pants that sat so low on her hips, I don't know how she kept them up. By the time we reached the red carpet she had stopped scowling. That woman just isn't happy unless she's killed a demon.

We get out of the limo and the paparazzi go insane. Cameras flashing everywhere. Blinding. Zane tried to stop, but it was too much of a security risk. Simone had one arm and I had the other. We paused for three seconds and then we pushed through the crowd and into the theater.

It was the El Capitan, which has been redone and is gorgeous inside. The beautiful and rich décor was the highlight of my evening. After that it went downhill like an avalanche of shit.

Thankfully, we arrived only about fifteen minutes before the film started. That meant a minimum amount of schmoozing with the beautiful people.

There were three actresses who fawned all over Zane. And I do mean all over. One of them had her hand on his crotch while she whispered in his ear.

The movie, if you could call it that, was supposed to be an action film about a ghost hunter with special psychic skills. Lame, lame, lame. Kira sitting on a stool telling stories about the dead people who keep bugging her would have been much more entertaining.

The only thing that kept me awake was Simone throwing popcorn in my face every few minutes. Normally it would have annoyed me beyond belief, but basically it kept me from being too bored.

Afterward, everyone stood up and applauded. I rolled my eyes. The director moved up on the stage and said something about how creatively challenging the project had been and how organic the story was. I don't know what's so organic about lame ghost hunters, but there you go. Then he brought the actors onstage. The hero was played by a gorgeous guy. I can't remember his name, but his eyes were bedroomy blue. He reminded me of the guy in the club but different.

The next thing I knew we were being led out of a side door and into the limo. It was only nine thirty, but I was exhausted.

Then Zane announced we were going to a party.

"No!" Simone and I yelled in unison.

"It isn't safe." I tried to soften my voice. "Zane, we explained this before."

"I know, I know. But it's at Harry Stein's house. He's an old friend and a producer of the film. I can't not go. The man owns half of Hollywood. Come on, we'll only stay for an hour. I promise."

Simone frowned and I shook my head.

"It's too risky." I sighed. I knew I'd give in but I had to try. He was a grown man and if he wanted to go to a party I couldn't stop him. I could advise against it, but couldn't stop him.

"Bronwyn, I have to go." He crossed his arms like a petulant child. So much for acting grown-up.

I turned and looked out the window.

We were driving high into the Hollywood Hills. The view was amazing. The lights twinkled and everything looked so beautiful.

But I knew it was all an illusion. This whole place was. Under those twinkling lights was a lot of evil. I'd seen it yesterday in that house where the demons had fed. I can see why Simone gets burned out every six months or so.

It isn't just here. Evil lives everywhere and some days it's fucking overwhelming.

When I turned back around Simone stared at me. She shook her head as if she knew what I was thinking. I smiled.

We don't always agree with one another, but we definitely understand each other.

Harry Stein's house was a monstrosity of glass and steel jutting out the side of the mountain. All of the lights were on and it was like a bright beacon.

A bright beacon for the false and pretentious.

I gotta say, I've never appreciated my new home in Sweet more than I do in this moment.

My guess is if I were home, I wouldn't have been propositioned by a demon to carry his children.

Let me explain.

Minutes after we arrived, Zane was wrapped around some blonde who caught his attention. "I've been such a good boy. I need to play." He smiled and rolled his eyes.

I pointed to his amulet. "Keep that on, and wear a condom."

He laughed as he walked away.

Simone disappeared soon after.

I sat on a barstool in a corner keeping watch over the room. Sipping my Pellegrino, I watched the rather intense interplay among the guests.

Two beautiful women stood close to Harry, wanting desperately to get his attention. I could see it in their eyes. I didn't need to read their minds.

He was surrounded by a group of men with cigars, all of whom had a glass of amber cognac in their hands.

The women kept whispering, finally in a fit of what had to be desperation, they started making out with one another. The men turned to watch. Harry smiled. His large belly jiggled with laughter. My stomach lurched at that smile. It was the grin of a predator. He touched one woman's shoulder and she stopped frenching the blonde. Then they both took Harry's arms and walked into a room on the left. Yuck. The visual of those girls going down on Harry was not a pretty one.

Oh, but the night was young.

Many of the groups were talking. The ones out by the pool seemed to be more relaxed and less business-oriented.

I made my way out and that's when I ran into him.

Gorgeous. Blue eyes and a body that was so taut and tight, I bounced right off of him. Entranced by a threesome in the pool, I didn't notice the cute guy until I ran into him.

I smacked against his chest and he grabbed my arms to keep me from falling in the pool.

"Sorry." I shrugged. "I'd say I didn't see you, but you're kind of hard to miss." I pointed to the pool. "I was a little distracted."

That made him laugh. "I can see why. They seem to be quite, um, close."

He put out his hand. "I'm Jason."

I must have been mistaken, about seeing him in the club. It couldn't have been the same guy.

We shook. "Bronwyn."

"Is this your first Hollywood party?" He had a nice smile.

I was mesmerized by his eyes. Even in the darkness I could see tiny orange flecks in the blue. Never seen anything like it.

"More or less. I've been to events out here with clients, but nothing like this."

It seemed like everywhere I looked people were making out. Bodies intertwined and so much kissing.

I turned back to him. "It's a bit much."

"Yes, I suppose it would be. You said clients. What's your business?"

Now see, I just don't tell everyone I'm a witch. And I knew if I said consultant he'd ask what kind. Everyone out here is a consultant of some kind.

"I'm in security."

"Oh, are you on Zane's detail? I watched you come in with him and the dark-haired woman."

He'd seen us, but I hadn't noticed him at all. Huh. "Um, yes I'm protecting Zane. What do you do?" Hey, I can make small talk with the best of them. Not really, but I felt like I was at least holding up my end.

He smiled and my heart dipped in my chest. God, the man was beautiful.

"I'm a breeder."

"Huh. Like horses?"

"No."

"Dogs?"

"No."

This was too weird. What else was there? Maybe he had a farm with special kinds of cows. Living where I did I'm surrounded by cows, but I don't know much about them.

I threw up my hands. "Okay, I give up. What do you breed?"

"These." He unbuttoned his shirt. I didn't have time to think about what he was doing.

Then his stomach split open and there were about fifty slimy eggs attached in a tiny sac.

I backed away from him. He was a demon and I hadn't even sensed it.

He moved toward me. "Don't be afraid, they won't hurt you. I only need to inseminate you and you won't feel a thing."

Um, ewwww. I held up a hand. "First of all stop where you are, or I'll kill you. Second, if I want to be inseminated, and I don't, it won't be by some creepy demon guy with a sack full of eggs."

He looked more offended than angry.

"It is a great honor to carry my children."

Okay, gross.

"Maybe where you come from, but here it's just disgusting. I'm asking you nicely to please leave me alone. In fact it would be better if you just left altogether. I hear there's a demon slayer here and she's been itching for a kill all night."

Never in my life had I wanted to zap someone with a fireball so bad, but I didn't think Zane would appreciate me killing someone at Harry's party.

His face became a mask. "Until later." Then he turned and left. I'm in the bathroom right now, and have just finished throwing up.

I'm going to find Zane and Simone and we are getting the hell out of this place. I can't imagine Simone's demon radar is down. This house has to be shielded by magic, and if that's the case we're going to have a tough time telling the good guys from the bad.

Twenty-four

Tuesday, 11 P.M.

Sleepy witches: 1

The good news is I've had another long rest. About forty-eight hours.

The bad news is that once again I almost died. And I feel like I could sleep another two days.

When I last wrote, I was hiding in Harry's bathroom at possibly the worst party I've ever been to. I ran out of there in search of Zane. I was about to give up when I found him in front of a fireplace making out with the blond chick we'd met at the door.

"Bronwyn, love, come meet Marni."

I gritted my teeth but gave her a quick wave. Then turned my attention back to Zane.

"Look," I pointed to the door, "we've got to get out of here now. Have you seen Simone?"

"No, and I don't want to leave. Marni and I are having a great time."

I closed my eyes but I didn't have time to count to ten. The effects of way too much alcohol glazed his eyes. Coherent conversation was impossible.

I grabbed his collar and pulled him up by the scruff. "Zane. We. Have. To. Go."

He patted my head like a puppy. "Okay, okay. Don't yell, luv." His words slurred. "I'm coming." He laughed. "Well, not yet, but Marni will help with that, won't you, darling girl?"

The blonde nodded and grabbed him by the waist. "I'll take him home," she offered. I hadn't noticed before but she really was beautiful. Something about her eyes made me think I'd seen her before, but I couldn't imagine where.

"I don't think that's a good idea. We need to follow our security protocol."

Zane laughed. "Come on Bron, look at her. She's gorgeous; we're just going to have a bit a fun. I promise we'll go straight to the house."

Patience isn't one of my virtues but I tried to stay calm. "Fine, she can come with us. But we will all ride together. Now stay here, I've got to find Simone."

I sent my mind out, but I couldn't find her anywhere. Damn. Opening doors, I made my way down one hallway and then another. Drunken people do some pretty weird crap in Hollywood.

It got to where I'd squeeze my eyes closed, worried about what I'd see next. When I walked in on Harry and his girls, I almost threw up for the second time that night. Gross.

Eventually, I found Simone in the pantry in the kitchen. She was so involved I couldn't see the guy's face at first. I grabbed her shoulder and pulled her away.

She whipped around. "Do you want to die—Oh, hey, Bron. This is James." Oh Lord, she was making out with one of the most famous actors in Hollywood in Harry's pantry.

"Sorry to interrupt, but we have a security issue." I continued to pull her out of the pantry.

"Damn, Bron, okay okay." She started to walk out and then turned back to the pantry. James stood there in a daze. She kissed him hard. Then said, "Call me," and stuck her card in his pocket.

I dragged her to the living room where I'd left Zane and the woman. They weren't there.

Made my way to the front door with Simone in tow.

"Have you seen Zane?" I asked the valet and handed him a twenty to get our limo.

"He left a few minutes ago with a blonde. Are you Bronwyn?"

"Yes."

"Yeah, he said he'd see you at home." The valet smiled and then took off in search of our limo.

Great. Fucking great.

Simone and I climbed in the limo and the driver pulled out on the narrow hillside road. I told her about what had happened with the demon.

"I think that's why they've been after me. A witch would be the perfect host for their demon seed. Whatever powers I have they would absorb. But I don't know if he was an Arnok or not. In human form it was hard to tell."

She grimaced. "You should have let me kill him. The bastard.

I'm sorry you don't seem to be having much fun. Except for Sir David you've had a pretty crappy time."

"I know." I grunted. "But it honestly wouldn't have been much better at home. Sam's mad and I don't know if I can fix it. Still, I can't wait to get back to Sweet."

That's when everything gets fuzzy.

I'm not sure but I think they must have used something in the air-conditioning vents. Before I realized what was happening, I saw Simone pass out. I wasn't far behind.

When we woke up we were in the middle of a dungeon or a basement that looked like one. A basement in California is a rarity, but I didn't feel so lucky to have found myself in one.

"Two weeks of sipping raspberry margaritas and mojitos on the beach. No worries, just sun and fun." I shifted on the dirt floor. The smell of dead rats overwhelmed my senses. I couldn't face Simone. The chains binding us to the steel pole wouldn't allow much movement.

"I know." The demon slayer sighed.

"I'm taking time off and we'll do nothing but fun girly things. Spa days, tanning, a trip to the hair salon to see Sir David, he's a master with highlights." I bit my lip and looked up at the ceiling. Nothing there that would help us.

"He is." The chains rattled. "And you're beautiful. Your hair's never looked better."

I ignored the compliment. "Sleep as much as you want."

"Well, there was that first day." Her voice carried an edge.

"I was shot with a tranquilizer dart." I tried to grab the chain with my hand, but was bound too tight.

"Yes, but you slept like a baby for twenty-four hours." She had the nerve to giggle.

"Get away from all of your troubles at home and experience how the Hollywood set lives. See the sights, and hang with the real *party crowd*," I grumbled. I couldn't help it.

"We were at a great party before this happened, and that one guy totally wanted in your pants."

"Yes, a demon who wanted to impregnate me with slime-filled eggs." I knocked on the pole with my fist. "This so sucks."

"Yep."

The door burst open. "Who is the first to die?" the demon roared. Stupid creep was way too dramatic. That's Hollywood for you.

I guess it was time.

"I'll go. Anything is better than listening to her bitch." Simone slid halfway up the pole.

"Simone?"

"What?"

The demon unshackled her chains. He smelled like dog pee. I suppose that was his natural aroma. At the party his body odor hadn't been so offensive. But, he'd been masking as a human.

"If we get out of this, I'm going to kick your ass." No levity in my voice.

"You'll have to wait in line. And I'd like to remind you, the assholes waiting upstairs are after you."

I cleared my throat. Damn, I'd guessed they were warlocks. Simone's senses confirmed it. "True. I'm sorry. None of this is your fault." It really wasn't. I tend to get in a bad mood when doom is near. I couldn't keep the worry from my voice. "I didn't mean it, before. You know that, right?"

She half laughed. "I know, Bron. It's not your fault either."

"Enough talk. Come, demon slayer. The master waits." His

big horned head motioned my way. "I'm going to enjoy watching you squirm, witch."

Can't believe I thought that jerk was cute at the party. He pulled Simone up the stairway and I smelled the smoke from the fire as he opened the door.

Man, I hate it when bad guys sacrifice my friends. And I especially hate the fact I'm next.

It didn't help that there were rats everywhere. I hate rodents. Really, really hate them.

A big fat gray one got way too close to the hem of my pants. I used the heel of my Jimmy Choo to impale him and then kicked him into his friends. The rats went into a screeching frenzy.

But they weren't loud enough to drown out Simone's screams. She never screams. I'd seen her with her arm nearly bitten off by a demon and she hadn't even whimpered.

The scream sent me into a panic. Those bastards were killing my friend.

I threw everything I had into my powers but nothing worked. They'd bound them tight.

I remembered what Garnout had said about calming myself. Then I whispered his name.

"Bronwyn." He came to me in a vision. "What's happened?" I told him the short version.

"I'm in the middle of my own battle." Hence his distracted look. "I'm sending you strength, my dear. My strength should allow you to break the spell and use your powers. It may make you dizzy at first, but you must move fast, for it won't last long."

"Thanks." I shook my head. My stomach roiled and I tried to breathe. Closing my eyes, I listened as he whispered a chant.

The energy tingled within me. Then I saw it, the magic that

bound me. I cut it with my mind using a metaphysical blade. I didn't know if it had been Garnout, or my own gifts. It didn't matter.

Using my new power, I shook the earth.

The idiots upstairs yelled, "Earthquake."

"No, it's something much, much worse." I gritted my teeth. The pole fell sideways and the chains slid off my body.

I heard more screams, but this time it wasn't Simone. It was a man.

Running up the stairs I hit the door with a fireball.

Power surged through me and I took the scene in. Five warlocks stood to the side over an altar. Simone was in the corner of the room doing her best to destroy that cute demon from the party. Good for her. The demon screamed. Simone's very good at her job.

Turning my attention to the warlocks I raised my arms. They didn't seem to care. They continued chanting. Over the altar I saw a wisp of energy rising. Whomever they were bringing forth I didn't want to meet.

I threw the first fireball at the one in the middle. It bounced off. They were protected by black magic.

But now I had mine and Garnout's powers to play with, and they didn't have a clue. I sent my mind into the one in the middle again. His orange eyes glowed bright and then he threw out his hands.

"You cannot harm us, witch. We bring forth our master. He protects us."

I stomped my foot and the earth shook again. The altar fell and one of the candles toppled onto the head of the warlock who spoke.

His master be damned, his cloak caught fire. The other war-locks were distracted trying to put the fire out on their comrade. They stopped chanting.

Simone had finished off the demon. The body stumbled around without a head and then fell to the floor. Can't say I was sorry to see him and those slimy eggs of his go.

"The two on the end are mine," she said under her breath. She was bleeding from her chest and wrists, but it didn't seem to bother her at the moment.

I concentrated first on the warlock who was on fire. Grabbing the altar knife they'd used on Simone, I used my mind to throw it directly into his heart.

He turned to ash.

Simone let out a war whoop and I saw her slicing with one of the knives she carried in back of her bustier. She started with his balls and slid the knife up.

A warlock, the one who had been next to ash boy, jumped on me. I hadn't been ready for that kind of physical attack. I jammed my knee up to his nads, but he caught it before I caused any harm.

Then I stuck my fingernails in his eyes. Totally messed up my manicure but it was worth it to hear him scream like a girl. I needed to remember to thank Simone for the self-defense lesson she'd given me years ago.

Before I could get up on my knees, the blinded warlock threw a pile of black sludge at me and I couldn't move in time. I felt it seep in to my bloodstream. But I refused to give in to it.

It sucks the energy out of you and makes you weak almost instantly, but I wouldn't let these assholes get the best of me. This was a fight to the death, and it wouldn't be me going to hell this time.

I threw a fireball. It landed to the right of him.

Out of the corner of my eye I saw Simone rise up. She'd finished off one warlock. We only had two left. But I couldn't see the other one.

"Bronwyn, move," Simone yelled.

Problem was, I didn't know which way. I ducked, but not before I got a knife in the shoulder.

"Fuck," I yelled.

She flew across the room and kicked the warlock in the gut.

I concentrated on the one I'd blinded. He had to suffer.

"I hate this fucking black sludge." I slammed a fist into his face.

He grabbed his bloodied nose. Then the asshole had the nerve to spit at me. I moved before his nasty blood hit me, but it really pissed me off.

I grabbed the knife from my shoulder. I should have passed out from the pain, but I wouldn't give in.

I jammed the blade into his heart.

"I go to my master, but he'll come for you, witch," the warlock screamed out before he turned to ash.

"I can't wait," I said to the pile of dirt at my feet.

Turned around to find Simone with her arm around the neck of the warlock. She had one of his ears in her mouth. Spitting it out, she screamed at him. "Where the fuck are those demons?"

"Topanga," he whispered, just before she broke his neck.

"I fucking hate warlocks. They're such pussies." She stood up. A gaping hole the size of a small fist was in the middle of her chest, and blood poured out.

I sent a healing spell to her.

She grabbed my hand. "Come on, we've got to get out of here before we both pass out."

We found a sedan with the keys in it, in front of the large house where they'd taken us.

I don't know how we made it to Malibu but we did.

That's where we found Zane tied to the bedposts.

Twenty-five

Sleepy witches: 1

The wards on the Malibu house had been broken. I knew as soon as we pulled up in the driveway.

By this time, neither Simone nor I were standing too well on our own. We half carried each other into the house.

I sent my mind to Zane and was relieved to see he was still alive. We found him in his bedroom, naked and tied to the bedposts.

His face was covered with tears, but he seemed unharmed. We ran to him, checking him over and untying the scarves that held his arms.

"Are you okay?" My voice was hoarse from all the screaming.

"Oh luvs, sit down. You both look like hell." He picked up the phone and dialed 911.

Simone grabbed the phone and turned it off. "No cops. There's no way we can explain what happened to Bron and me."

Zane rubbed his wrists where the scarves had been. "My God, what happened?"

"We'll tell you later, we don't have the energy for it now. What happened to you?"

Zane shook his head. "First, I need you to look in on Zoë and make sure she's okay."

Honestly, I wasn't sure I had the strength, but I had to. From the look in his eyes, something terrible had happened.

I grabbed his hand, and had him look in my eyes again.

"Zoë?"

She looked up. Standing by a window in her nightgown, she stared at me. "Bronwitch, is Uncle Zane okay?"

"Yes, honey." I turned so she could see him. "He's right here."

Her tiny body shivered with relief. "Oh, Uncle, I was so scared when I saw the bad lady with you."

"I'm okay, Poppet. She wasn't going to hurt me. She was only scared."

She cried, and the tears fell on Zane's face too. "Honey, you're coming to America."

She smiled through her tears. "Is the bad lady gone?"

"Yes, baby. She can't scare you anymore. I promise."

"Zane," I whispered, "I can't hold it much longer."

"Little luv, Uncle has to go but I'll see you tomorrow. I'm sending the plane for you right now."

"I love you."

"Love you too, baby."

I closed my eyes. I could feel the sludge sliding into my system.

"Tell me what happened, but make it fast. Where's the bad lady?"

He sighed. "She wasn't bad. And her name is Marni. She's Zoë's mom."

My eyes flew open, and I heard Simone's sharp intake of breath.

"She'd been trying to get Zoë back and she made a deal with some demon with a B name. I can't remember exactly what she said. He promised her baby back if she served him."

Probably Blaseus.

His body shook and a small sob escaped. He pushed the emotion back. Showing incredible strength, he continued.

"She planned all of this, to kill me in my own home. I don't know if she was directly responsible for the death of my brother, but she was involved.

"She lured me into bed. It wasn't hard. I was wasted. I noticed something strange about her eyes and at first I thought maybe she'd drugged me. It looked as though her eyes were on fire."

Oh, wow, that meant possession. The same as the warlocks.

"I was tied up before I realized she meant me real harm. She had the knife above her head ready to plunge it into me. Then she looked at me strangely. My amulet was glowing so bright it almost blinded me."

He pushed himself up on the headboard.

"Her whole body shook and then her eyes changed back to normal and she wailed. It was a horrible sound. That's when Zoë suddenly showed up over my shoulder. She yelled at the woman. She was so fierce. 'Get away, bad lady, go away. Or the Bronwitch will kill you.' That's when Marni really broke down.

"Marni's head dropped to her chest. 'Send her away, send her away, I won't hurt you.' She dropped the knife. And little Zoë disappeared. Oh, the name of the demon was Blackstock. The one she made the deal with. I remembered because I used to have a guitar player with that name. He left to start his own band. Wonder what happened to that guy?"

The name made me choke. "What did you say?"

"He left to start his own band."

I rolled my eyes and grunted. "No, the name. Are you sure?"

"Yes, I'm sure that was it. He'd promised her that if she helped him, she would get her baby back. But seeing Zoë did something to her. She ran off right before you got here and I haven't seen her since."

That's when I realized Marni might still be in the house. I looked at Simone and we both pushed off the bed. She checked Zane's closet and I went into the bathroom.

That's where I found her. She couldn't have been more than twenty-five. My age. That meant she was a teen when Zoë was born.

At first I couldn't tell what happened, but she was prone on the floor, barely breathing. Her blond hair was a tangled mess, and she still wore the clothes she had on at the party. I motioned to Zane and Simone and they followed me in. I slid to the floor and took her hand. Her pulse was almost nonexistent.

"Tell Zoë, her mommy loves her." A tear slid down her cheek. "I'm so sorry." Then she stared at the ceiling, lifeless. I tried to throw my healing powers into her, everything I had. But it was useless. She wanted to die and she was gone.

In her hand we found a handful of small green pills. I sniffed them. Belladonna. In small doses it helps you sleep, in larger amounts the sleep is more permanent. Her purse was open on the counter, and she'd gone through it quickly to find the herbs she wanted.

There was a large bang downstairs and I pulled myself up by the cabinet and stood ready. Saying a small prayer that it wasn't more demons and warlocks, I almost cried when the prime minister and Azir rounded the corner of the bathroom.

I smiled. "It's about time." And that's the last I remember. I woke up and looked at my watch and it's Tuesday. I've been out for two days.

Oh, Azir's coming to see me. I can feel him. Zane told me earlier that Azir's spent the last forty-eight hours looking after me. They called in Simone's shaman friend Roy to help detoxify my system from the black sludge.

I didn't know anything. I've been in a serious REM state the whole time.

Kind of hoped someone had told Sam, but if they did, he obviously didn't care enough to even call. Whatever.

Good, Azir is here. I need to thank him.

Twenty-six

Wednesday, 11 A.M.

Wards: 1

Spells: 3

Witches who are ready to go home: 1

Azir was nothing but sweet to me. A complete turnaround from the way he acted in New York. I was a little embarrassed when I found out he'd watched me sleep the last two days.

Dressed in jeans, an opened white button-down and sandals, he looked California chic. Kind of cool for a Middle Eastern sheik.

"You look much better this morning." He had a tray with him.

Now, let me take a moment and just settle this in my head. I'm in the world's most famous rock star's house, being served breakfast by one of the richest men in the world.

My life really isn't so bad.

"Thank you. But I think I could use a toothbrush and maybe a shower. You might want to stay by the door." I smiled.

He laughed and he didn't listen to my warning. "I'll take my chances." Setting the tray on my lap, he pulled a chair up next to the bed.

"We were anxious there for a few minutes. The shaman was worried we'd waited too long to treat you. Simone told him that if he let you die, he wouldn't have anything to worry about because he'd be dead. Let's just say he worked well under pressure." I'd forgotten how much I liked Azir's smile.

I giggled. I love Simone. "Is she doing okay? She had some nasty stab wounds."

"She was covered with blood but refused treatment until she knew for sure you'd be fine. She's quite fearless, that one. You two make a good team."

"She's definitely that, and yes we do. Um, thanks for looking after me. I know you must have a million things to do."

He shrugged. "I wanted to be here. Beyond all of this, you are my friend."

I picked up a piece of toast from the tray. Awkward. There's no better word for this particular scenario. I still had feelings for Azir. More than friendship feelings, but not at all like what I felt for Sam.

I offered him the other piece and he took it. "Azir, if I ask you a question will you answer me honestly?"

He chuckled. "It depends on the question." His intense stare made me shiver.

"Was Sam with you last week?"

He nodded.

"You don't have to tell me the specifics, but did anything happen to him?"

"No, not that I know of. It was a difficult mission and there were many children involved. We were transporting them from the Philippines to a safe house. That's all I can tell you."

"Oh. Okay. But nothing happened?"

"Not out of the ordinary. Why, did something happen between you and Sam?"

This was the last person I should discuss my man troubles with, but he would probably have the best perspective. He did love me once.

"I called him while you were on the mission and a woman answered his phone. I suspected the worst, because well, I'm me. Later he told me the phone had been stolen."

I sighed. "Then there was an unfortunate mix-up and he thought Zane and I were sleeping together."

Azir's eyebrows rose. "Were you?"

"We didn't fool around but we did pass out in the same bed. Sam found out, and he won't listen to reason. But there's something beyond his being jealous. I don't know. He hasn't been himself since the attack a few months ago." The words fell out of my mouth like an uncontrolled waterfall. I couldn't stop talking.

He reached and took my hand. "Bronwyn, it's difficult for a man to be in a relationship with you."

I tried to give him my evilest stare.

Holding up a hand in surrender, he continued. "You are often in precarious situations, and everything is life and death. It's difficult for a man whose natural instinct is to protect you to deal with this.

"And the fact that you were in bed with a man known for his

prowess with women wouldn't be an easy thing for anyone to understand. It doesn't matter that it was innocent. Certainly, this is not difficult to comprehend?"

I circled my head around, trying to release the tension in my neck. "I do understand it. But he knows I love him and wouldn't do anything to hurt him. Well, I keep doing things, but I don't mean to."

He laughed again. "Like I said, loving you isn't always easy. He loves you, Bronwyn. How could he not? You are beautiful, intelligent and one of the most powerfully endearing women I've ever met."

His words made a tear fall to my cheek.

Reaching up with his thumb, he wiped it away.

"What you have to decide is if you are willing to meet him halfway. Do you want to fight for Sam? Maybe you don't love him as much as you think you do."

A sob came out of my throat and he stood. He moved the tray and then sat down, taking me in his arms as he did.

"Yes. I love him, Azir. I do, so much I can't stand it."

"This, my love, is why I didn't fight harder for you. Your love for him is deep. Love like this doesn't come along often, and you should fight for it with everything you have."

I blubbered against his chest. His scent was a blend of spicy cologne and powerful man. An intoxicating combination. Taking a breath, I pushed away.

I stared at his rich brown eyes, and those illegally long lashes. It would be so easy to love this man. But my heart belonged to Sam.

"If you love him so much, Bronwyn, then get mad. You aren't the kind of woman who sits around whining. You go after what you want."

"I *will* go after what I want. I have to get home. I wish I didn't have to wait for this stupid concert on Saturday. Well it's not stupid, but you know what I mean."

He hugged me. "That may happen sooner than you think."

Garnout walked in. I wondered where he'd been. Usually when I'm hurt he's first on the scene. I'd been surprised when I heard the shaman was the one to help heal me.

"Greetings, young witch."

I nodded toward him.

Azir stood. "I'll leave you now."

Garnout motioned for him to sit down. "No need, I can only stay for a moment." He put a hand on my head and said a chant.

The wizard lifted my chin with his fingers. "You're healing. Shaman Roy did well."

I'd yet to meet this Shaman Roy, but evidently he had the metaphysical healing arts down to a science. But I have to admit Roy seemed an odd name for one so powerful.

"Your friend Caleb will be here in the morning to take you back to Sweet." Garnout sat on the side of the bed. "Until you've fully healed, you'll be of little use here."

"But—" How could I do my job if he sent me home? There were thousands of people to protect at the concert.

He laughed. "Your poker face needs work, Bronwyn. No one is usurping your powers. But Zane no longer needs your protection. There are several local covens here who will join to protect the arena for the concert." He held up a hand. "No, you could do it better, but I'll pop in to make sure everything runs as it should. We feel now, with the girl gone, and the warlocks you and Simone killed, the threat is diminished."

He cleared his throat, and put his hand my head again. "Yes, you'll be fine, but you need at least two weeks of peace and quiet."

My life in Sweet was slower, but seldom peaceful or quiet.

"It feels wrong to leave the job again before it's completed. I was sent home early from London, and it just doesn't look good."

Zane walked in. My room had become Spago on a Friday night in the old days. Wolfgang Puck would be jealous.

He waved a hand. "Don't be gormless, luv. You've saved my life so many times in the last few weeks you deserve an award. Go home and take care of yourself."

I put my hands on my hips. "What is this, boss Bronwyn day?"

"I want to see the Bronwitch," a child whispered outside in the hallway.

"Bring her in, Georgette," Zane called to them.

His assistant came around the corner with the tiny girl on her hip. Zoë's big eyes looked at me in wonder. Her little hand went up in a tiny wave.

"Hi, Bronwitch," she whispered. Then she giggled.

The sound made me smile.

"Hello, my brave friend, Zoë. I see you've come to see Uncle Zane."

She wiggled to be put down on the end of the bed. She was dressed in a bright blue jumper and white blouse. With her black Mary Janes, she looked like a tiny fairy schoolgirl.

"Yes, and I'm going to get to stay forever." She drew out the last word with her arms opening wide.

Zane reached down and picked her up. He swung her in a circle. "That's right. Poppet and me, well, we're a full-time team now."

I couldn't help laughing. They both seemed so happy.

Zane's face turned serious. "Go home, Bronwyn. Heal. Then you can come play with us again."

Zoë held out her hand. "Wait, if the Bronwitch goes I can't see her."

"Don't worry, I'll still check on you, and remember when you wear that necklace all you have to do is say my name."

That made her smile. "Okay." She turned to Zane. "I think I want a pony."

Everyone in the room laughed.

I bet she gets the horse. That little girl is going to be a powerful witch one day.

So now, I'm packing up.

I can't wait to get home.

Twenty-seven

Thursday, noon
Sweet, Texas
Spells: 0
Potions: 2

There isn't anything like waking up in your own bed, with your stuff surrounding you. There's a completeness about it. And it's one of the things that makes me happy.

Kira stopped by with tea and breakfast this morning. She's feeling much better about her new abilities and says there are more dead people than live ones in Sweet.

"Thank God you taught me how to see auras." She laughed. "You'd be surprised how many dead people hang out at the Piggly Wiggly. It's hard not to talk to them, especially when they insist on talking to me, but I'm learning."

I pulled a muffin filled with blueberries out of the bag. The smell of fresh baked goods, yum. "Maybe you should hang a shingle out at the library and make appointments for all the dead folks."

She nearly spat tea, she laughed so hard. "Okay, the sad thing is, I actually thought about it. I feel like I'm supposed to be helping them. Most of them just have the oddest questions like, 'How's Eldon doing? I haven't seen him in years.' Of course I don't have a clue who they're talking about."

"Have you told Caleb yet?"

She looked down at her hands. "No. I will, though. Soon."

"Um, you might think about doing it really soon. He thinks you're having an affair." I bit my lip to keep from laughing. The whole situation was so absurd.

This time she did spit. She jumped up to grab a paper towel from the cabinet. "What would make him think such a thing?"

"Well, on the way home from L.A. yesterday, he told me you were in the bathroom whispering to someone. You've been coming home late, and you act like you're hiding something."

She sighed. "I'd laugh if it weren't so sad. I'll tell him tonight."

I wanted to ask her about Sam, but we never got around to it. She had to run off to the library. I'm so lame, I called and left a message this morning that if he wanted to talk, I was back.

Haven't heard a peep.

Friday, 2 P.M.
Soon to be fat witches without a boyfriend: 1
I'm going to become a lesbian. I bet Kira has a book about it in the library.

That's it. I hate men. They're fucked up in the worst way.

Sam sucks.

There. I said it and the world didn't explode. Though my stomach may if I eat any more of these Sno Balls. Why am I so passionate about pink, coconut-covered chocolate cupcakes? It's a sick obsession. Better cupcakes than men. Cupcakes don't rip your heart out of your chest and stomp on it with five hundred dollar shoes. Oh, that's Zane. Sam's shoes probably only cost a hundred.

I hate him. Did I mention that?

I decide to drive by his office. I'm a sick witch. I need to be checked out. I go in and his nurse says he's busy with a patient.

"No problem, I'll just sit out here." Normally she would have sent me back to the office to wait for him. That's okay. So, I wait and wait.

Finally, I see him crossing between exam rooms. He stops in the hallway and stares at me. Dressed in his lab coat, jeans and a light blue shirt, he looks amazing. I smile and wave.

His face is expressionless. But he nods and then turns and walks into the room.

A few minutes later, the phone rings. The nurse looks right at me. "Yes, yes. Okay." And she hangs up.

She smiles. That really nasty smile that people get right before they are going to say something mean. "Bronwyn, I'm sorry. But he really can't fit anyone else in today. I can make an appointment with Dr. Gray for you for tomorrow if you'd like."

I bit the inside of my lip to keep from saying what I really wanted to. I smiled. "No, thanks." I walked out.

Oh, I was so fucking mad at him. Too busy, my ass.

So, I go to Piggly Wiggly. A girl has got to have a Sno Balls cupcake when things like this happen. And my cupboards are really bare after being gone so long. I used to be addicted to iced sugar cookies, but I ate so many one day that they made me sick. Haven't been able to look at them since.

Margie's there at the grocery store. It's her day off. She accidentally pushes her basket into the canned green beans display and hugs me.

"I'm so glad you're home. Kira said you've had a rough time the last few weeks." She squeezed my hands in hers.

I couldn't help but smile. "I'm fine, Margie, but as always, very glad to be home. How's it going with your new man?"

She giggled like a little girl. "God, it's great. Like the most wonderful thing ever." Then she frowned. "Oh, I'm sorry. I shouldn't go on like this with—"

"With what?"

Margie stared at her shoes. "Um, well. The trouble with Sam, and him seeing that girl and all while you were away."

There was a sudden rumble in the store, and the cantaloupes and watermelons fell to the floor with giant clunks.

Closed my eyes and brought myself under control.

Margie had grabbed one of the shelves. "What the hell was that?"

I pretended I didn't know and shrugged my shoulders. "Well, I better be going. It was great to see you, Margie. Let's catch up soon." I ran to the checkout.

The cashier, being the intelligent woman that she was, didn't say a word about the six boxes of Sno Balls cupcakes, two gallons of rocky road, bottle of chocolate milk or the five bottles of wine that lined my basket. I did manage to remember cat litter and cat food, which in retrospect makes the whole thing even sadder.

So I go home and unload all the groceries. I stuff six cupcakes down my throat while I put it all away. If it hadn't been eleven in the morning I would have opened the wine.

Then I remembered what Azir said. That if I wanted Sam and if I really loved him, I had to fight for him.

I ran upstairs and changed clothes. But before I could start my plan, I needed some fried chicken from Lulu's. There's nothing better for a troubled mind or heart than fried chicken.

I felt so good when I stepped into Lulu's. I wore my gorgeous new jeans, and a Dolce and Gabbana scarf blouse with the Marc Jacobs Mary Janes. Okay, so I was a little overdressed for Sweet, but I didn't give a damn.

I'd even managed to get my hair to curl in a semblance of the same style Sir David had done. I looked damn good.

I saw Sam in the corner booth. He looked up when I walked in. His baby blues raking me from head to toe. I saw the lust in his eyes first, and a hint of love. I know the look, and it's one of my favorite things in the world. I adore turning him on.

When the woman across from him turned around, I wanted to throw up. She was beautiful. Long straight blond hair, and a face that was angelic. I hated her instantly.

Turning tail and running sounded like the best idea. But Ms. Johnnie, who had taken in the exchange from behind the counter, yelled, "Helen, get out here. The most beautiful girl in the world just walked in the door."

Helen came around the corner with a spatula. "Well, darlin', you are a sight for this old woman." She hugged me. It took everything I had not to sag in her arms and sob.

"You stand strong girl, and show what you're made of," Helen whispered in my ear. She may have been in the kitchen, but she hadn't missed anything.

"Oh, it's so good to see you both." I smiled. I'm sure my eyes were shiny with tears, but none fell. And I'm damn proud of that.

"You're here to pick up your order of fried chicken? Kira called and said you might be by. She says she can't get away for lunch and would you bring her some?" Johnnie had given me an out. A way I could run away and not look like the big loser I was.

"Yes, I'll take Kira her lunch. And you guys are going to have to start overnighting this chicken to me when I'm gone. Every time I leave town I go through withdrawals."

They both cackled. In a matter of seconds they had a giant bag of food ready to go.

"Don't be a stranger." Ms. Johnnie hollered as I was walking out. It took everything I had not to look back at Sam.

I didn't imagine Kira had called, but she was grateful for the meal.

"Bron, I saw him the other night with her, but I—" she touched my arm. "I didn't know what to think. Maybe she's just a friend. She doesn't live here, I know that."

We sat behind the large desk where she's set up her office in the library.

"I don't know what to do. Maybe I should let him move on. Azir said it best—it isn't easy being in a relationship with me."

Kira snorted. "That's bullshit. You are one of the kindest, most loyal people I've ever met. Yes, you do have habit of almost getting killed every few weeks, but you know we all have our faults."

I laughed out loud and hugged her.

"Thank you for being my friend."

"Well, what are you going to do?" She sipped her tea. "You gonna let that blond bimbo steal your man? She's the rebound girl. It'll never last."

I shook my head. "I don't know. But the way he looked at me—he wanted me."

"Fight for him, Bron. He hasn't been himself since you left the first time to go to London. Something's up. Maybe if you just sat down and talked, hashed it all out, you two could make it work."

"Maybe." I could just kill the bimbo. Well, maybe kill is too strong of a word. Serious maiming. Now that could work.

So now I'm at home stuffing my face. But I have to stop. Kira's right, I'm not going to let some blond bimbo ruin the best thing that's ever happened to me.

I love Sam, and I know we belong together.

I bet that's exactly what stalkers say. But I owe it to myself to at least give it a try.

Watch out, Sam. Here I come.

Twenty-eight

Charms: 1

Battle-ready witches: 1

I spent the morning preparing for battle. That's right. I made a list of all of Sam's favorite things. From my pink lacy Victoria's Secret panties to the red shirt with the V down to there. He loves vanilla, I'll bathe in it. High heels are huge turn-ons. I'll wear them.

This is a war of seduction, and I will win.

I'll make him forget all of the crap of the last few weeks. He'll know there's no other man for me, and that I'm all the woman he ever needs.

He will be mine.

Okay, that does sound a lot like a stalker, but there's a bucketload at stake here. And I refuse to give up.

I'm going to break into his house. That's one of the pluses of being a witch. It's really hard to keep us out if we want in.

I'll set up dinner, have candles going, the whole bit. He won't know what hit him, and when he sees what I'm wearing, the red shirt, the black leather mini, and four-inch heels, he'll drool. He may still throw me out, but he'll drool when he does.

God, I'm so nervous, it's sick. Fingers crossed.

I better start now if I want to look good by five. What if he has a date with her? He'll still have to come home and change, hopefully. And when he stands her up, well there ya go.

Please, God, don't let me make an idiot out of myself tonight.

Saturday, 1 A.M.

I'm in the kitchen, can't sleep and I don't want to ever forget this night.

I threw up twice before I drove to Sam's. God bless cinnamon Altoids. Thankfully, his door wasn't locked. One of the graces of living in a small town. I got everything set up, and then it was a matter of waiting.

I tried to send my mind out to his, just wanted to make sure that he wasn't already on a date with the other woman. The idea of it made me ill.

But his mind was slammed tight against mine.

I lit the candles and took a deep calming breath. I'd been in his house before, but I walked around like it was the first time. There were pictures of his parents on the side table. The art he adored, mostly modern abstracts, sat on the floor against the white walls.

The furniture was low and kind of a dark teal with red accents. He had the taste of a Manhattan designer. I swear. His mother, who is one of those ladies who lunch and never has a hair out of place, had definitely influenced him.

It was a small cottage house on the outside but looked like a Manhattan loft on the inside. He'd redone the kitchen with black granite, and stainless steel appliances. Very streamlined and beautiful.

When I heard the doorknob turn I closed my eyes.

"Here we go," I whispered.

He stopped just inside the door.

"Who's here?" His voice held a warning.

I came around the corner. "Don't shoot. It's me." I laughed.

He frowned. "What are you doing here?" The angry words were spat out.

I had to scrape my soul off the floor and put it back in my chest. I smiled. "I wanted to talk, and you've been so busy lately. I thought maybe we could just have dinner."

I pointed to the table. "I brought some food from Lulu's and thought we could, you know, act like grown-ups and discuss what's been going on."

He shook his head. "I told you I didn't want to talk." He turned to leave.

I didn't want to do it, but I had no choice.

Using my powers I pushed him up against the wall and held him there.

"I shouldn't do it this way, but you won't listen, so here it goes. I love you, Sam. I love you more than any one person I've ever known. I gave you my heart and soul. And I don't honestly know what more I can do to prove it to you."

I held up a hand. "I know what happened in London and L.A. didn't look good. I understand why you would be pissed off. But

I haven't slept with another man since I met you. Do you know why? Because I love you. I don't want anyone else. Zane is my friend and he will always be my friend. There are times when I'm going to work with him again. The same with Azir. But they are my friends. Nothing more. You, Sam. You are the man I love."

He stared, his face blank of emotion.

Fine, at least he'd have to listen to the rest.

"As for my job. I refuse to quit for you or anyone else. I don't like the fact that people keep trying to kill me any more than you do. In fact I hate it. But it's important to me. It's my way of sharing my gifts."

I put my hands on my hips. "Now, I don't know if you've been fucking around with that chick at Lulu's, but I'm willing to forgive you. I was willing to let you have the benefit of the doubt when some strange woman answered your cell phone last week. All I want to know from you is why the hell you can't do the same for me. You know me, Sam. I'm honest. I suck at relationships but I don't cheat. I don't lie, and I don't—except for trying to find sexy outfits that will drive you mad—play head games. I want to know how you can stop loving me because of what you think might have happened." I let go of the power.

It drained me more than I'd imagined. I obviously still needed to heal, but I refused to pass out. It was a matter of honor. I took a deep breath and waited for him to say something.

He didn't say a word.

Great. Fucking great.

I walked to the coffee table and picked up my purse. I didn't say a word, just walked to the door. I reached for the knob and he grabbed my hand. The energy from his touch sizzled up my arm.

I couldn't breathe.

He pulled me to him and just held me. Didn't talk. Just held tight. The heat from his body poured into mine. I sighed.

Kissing me, he ran his hands up and down my back. I ran mine through that gorgeous hair. Our tongues danced and I could feel him harden against my leg.

He moved us to the couch and I lay underneath him. Our bodies pressed hard into one another as if we were trying to become one.

Then something weird happened. My energy lagged. "Sam," I whispered. I thought I saw his eyes glow weird.

The next thing I knew I was in my own bed and he was lying next to me.

"What happened?"

"You passed out. My guess is you weren't ready to use your powers again. Did you drink your blue juice today, and take the herbals Garnout gave you?"

I'd been so busy planning his seduction that I'd forgotten. Great seduction. I'd passed out before we got to the good stuff. Still, he was in my bed. Fully clothed but in my bed.

He pushed my hair away from my face.

"You know, this isn't what I planned." I pushed myself up in the bed. "I was going to ravage your body so that you'd never forget me. Hey, how did you know about the herbals?"

"I called Garnout. He said to tell you the concert has gone off without a hitch and all is well. And I could never forget you, Bron. I've been trying but I just can't."

I wasn't really feeling up to this conversation, but we had to have it if we were going to move forward.

"I love you, Bron, more than I've ever loved anyone. You know my insecurities and my problems with trust. That isn't an excuse for the way I've acted, but dammit, you make trusting so hard sometimes. Every time you leave I honestly wonder if you are coming back. I guess more than trusting you with other men, it's trusting you to have the sense to survive."

I frowned. I didn't know what to say, because I really did understand how he felt.

Grabbing his hand, I squeezed. "So, tell me what it means, Sam. You were with that woman. Does that mean you want to move on, that this relationship is too much trouble?"

He sighed and pulled me into his arms. "No, you are a handful, but this relationship means more to me—I love you. I meant that when I said it. And as much as I tried I can't stop.

"As for the woman. She's an old friend. Not an old lover, just a friend. She was doing some research on small town medicine and the quality of care. I invited her here as a distraction. I needed someone to help me get over you, and she was convenient."

My heart skipped a beat and I wanted to ask if he slept with her, friend or not, but I couldn't do it. Whatever happened between them needed to stay in the past. Knowing wouldn't help what we were trying to build.

I rubbed his back with the tips of my fingers. "Are you feeling better? You've been acting strange for weeks. Not your normally happy self. And you can blame me if you want, but it started before I even left for New York."

He shrugged. "I don't know. I've been tired since the attack. I get headaches and sudden fevers. I've been doing tests on myself, but so far, nothing. My surgeons think it's a natural part of the body trying to heal itself. There was so much trauma—God, I've been looking through your magic books at various healing spells trying to see if I could find something to help."

A truck that Blackstock had thrown on him had crushed his body. If it hadn't been for the healing powers of the local coven, I don't think he would have survived.

I moved in his arms so I could see his face. I touched his cheek and moved my fingers across his lips. He kissed the tips. "Maybe we could recuperate together." I smiled. "We've both pushed ourselves too hard, too soon. We should take a vacation. Hey, how did you get me back here to the house?"

"I picked you up, threw you over my shoulder and brought you here. With that skirt, I'm sure we gave the neighbors an eyeful." He laughed. "But I know you heal better here. You were drained, and this house seems to work amazingly well at getting you back in your groove."

"It must. I'm feeling very much like grooving right now." I stretched out on top of him. He'd undressed me before he put me in bed, and had only left the pink panties.

"Are we going to make this work, Sam?" I whispered, still afraid he might say no.

"Yes, baby. We're going to make it work." He bent down and kissed me. His lips were tender, and then he nibbled on my bottom lip.

Rolling me over, he pressed himself between my legs. His jeans were rough on my skin, but I loved the feel of him.

Trailing kisses up my neck, he growled, "It was all I could do not to attack you while you slept. You know how much I love those panties."

I took his head in my hands and brought his lips to mine. "Yes, I do."

He slid his hand down inside the panties and touched my

heat. I was wet and ready. I didn't want foreplay. I wanted him inside of me.

Shaking his head, he smiled. He knew what I wanted but he was going to torture me in the most exquisite way.

I resigned myself and accepted his pleasure as his fingers danced up and down and in and out.

"Baby, please," I begged.

The room swirled around us in a haze of color. Purple, blue. Our magic mixed and I moaned again.

There was a strange energy in the room but I was so filled with pleasure, I couldn't think. Except to know that it was different.

I pushed against him enough so that he moved, and I could slide a hand to the outside of his jeans. His cock stretched the material tight. I carefully maneuvered my fingers so I could slide down his zipper. His shaft was in my hands and, this time, he moaned against my mouth.

He pulled the panties down and then shifted so I had to let him go.

Shoving his pants to the floor, he stood on the side of the bed. He grabbed my legs and wrapped them around his waist.

I shimmied my hips to get nearer to him. "Come on, baby. Please."

"Do you love me, Bronwyn?"

"Yes, more than anything."

He plunged into me and then moved within me at a mad pace. Without missing a thrust, he moved up to the bed on his knees, lifting my hips. I could take almost all of him this way and he knew I loved it.

I met his pace and watched his face. We couldn't get enough of each other.

"Sam." His name was said on a whisper of sheer pleasure. My body shook with orgasm.

"Stay with me." He thrust harder and faster. Shifting, he was over me now. My legs were still wrapped around his waist.

I opened my eyes and, as we came, I could have sworn his eyes flashed a strange color. But it could have been my own haze of lust. And our auras were off. When we mix our magic it's usually gold, but this was different. More of an orangey amber color. Weird.

I didn't think about it much then. I was spent and strangely energized at the same time, as if making love with him had healed something inside of me. Something the herbal remedies and blue juice couldn't.

He completes me. It's so corny it's funny, but it's true. I love him so much. I never want to forget this feeling. Never. He loves me just as much. I could feel it. When he came inside me that love filled me to overflowing.

I need to get back. I don't want him to wake up without me.

Twenty-nine

Sunday, 5 P.M.
Sweet, Texas
Spells: 4
Potions: 5
Bad guys: 1
Powerful witches: 1

*L*ove can kill. I'm living proof of it. I'd laugh if it weren't so messed up.

I'd been back in bed about two hours when I woke up. Heard something weird. I reached out to touch Sam, but Casper was curled up where he'd been.

Sat up and my eyes tried to adjust to the darkness.

Then I saw him.

Sam stood at the end of the bed.

"You okay, baby?"

I saw something flash in his eyes and then they burned orange. Fuck.

"Sam?" I edged myself back against the headboard.

"You thought you could defeat me, bitch. But you can't. I will kill you, and all of your powers will be mine." It wasn't Sam's voice, it was Blackstock's. I knew that stereo sound from before when the warlock had possessed Cole.

"We played this game last time, asshole, and I won."

"I'm much more powerful than before. You cannot win this game, witch." The knife flashed in his hand.

"The Blood Goddess took you, how could you have escaped her hell?"

His laugh was an evil sound that sent chills across my body.

"She sold my soul to Blaseus. The idiot demon was no match for someone like me. I slayed him in the pit, and his minions were forced to follow me. I will be even more powerful when I take your powers for my own."

Here's the thing: I could have thrown a fireball, but since he was born of fire, it wouldn't have done much good. He hadn't bound my powers. Probably didn't think he needed to. But I had a secret. He might be possessing Sam, but even Sam didn't know all of my powers.

I looked above his head. The large picture would work well.

He thrust out with the knife and moved forward.

"No!" I screamed. The room shook and he fell back. The picture fell from the wall and hit him on the head. He collapsed on the floor.

"Bronwyn, are you okay?" Kira yelled as she ran up the stairs, Caleb close on her heels.

She rounded the corner, her eyes flashing with surprise when she saw me standing naked over Sam's prone body.

Her hand flew up and she covered Caleb's eyes before he could see me.

"Caleb, go get some rope." I reached to the bedpost and grabbed my robe. "Kira, help me move him away from the wall. I don't know how much time we have. How did you know?"

Caleb came back in. "The dead people told her."

Didn't have time for any more questions, but I sent a quick blessing for Kira's new power. I couldn't do what I was about to on my own.

By the time we dragged him to the middle of the floor, Caleb was back with the ropes. They bound his wrists and feet while I threw on some jeans and a T-shirt.

I heard the front door slam. "Bronwyn?" It was Peggy from the coven.

"We're up here. Is Mike with you?"

"Yes, and Inspector Cole."

Cole? What the hell was he doing here?

Cole looked at me and nodded. "I knew when you left L.A. that it wasn't over. Don't know how, but I just knew it."

The men carried Sam downstairs and out to the back field. It was as if everyone knew their mission. More coven members showed up. In less than five minutes we had almost enough for a full circle.

Running back to the house to grab blue juice, I chugged it down. Using my powers in the way I was about to could kill me. I knew it, but I wouldn't let that bastard have my Sam.

Also pulled a bottle of naming potion, salt and Caiale potion for later, if we survived this.

Peggy used the salt to complete the circle. We were still a few members short.

I turned to Caleb and Kira. "We need you. It's a lot to ask and what you will see won't be pretty—in fact it's about to get very scary out here."

"Shut up, Bron, and just do what you need to." Caleb's voice was harsh. "He's our friend too."

I nodded.

Cole stood at the head of the circle. That worried me because, like Sam, Blackstock had touched him. That's how the bastard had zoned in on him. Some small part of the evil warlock's sludge had to have been hiding in Sam's body.

I'd read a lot about possession. I never wanted to get caught in that situation again. I'd also discussed with Garnout the best way to rid someone of a demon possession. While Blackstock was a warlock, he'd killed a demon and absorbed those powers too.

Didn't matter. I had it covered.

I just didn't know if Sam or I would die first.

"Bronwyn, the circle's ready," Cole yelled.

"Switch places with Peggy. I don't want to take any chances."

He looked confused for a minute then nodded. He knew his body could be used as a vessel for evil if there were any mistakes.

Peggy held up her arms. The coven linked hands and began the chant. Caleb and Kira followed their words carefully.

I did the same. Standing at Sam's feet, I drew a circle with the salt and then a mental one. He was still unconscious, and I prayed he stayed that way. This would be painful for both of us.

I closed my eyes and willed the Goddess of Earth forward. She's my goddess to call and I needed all the power I could get.

"I ask thee to cleanse the soul of this demon breath. Make this man whole again."

The winds picked up and swirled around us. The awful smell of sulfur filled the air. Blackstock was fighting back.

Sam's eyes flashed open. "Bron?" But it was Sam this time, not the warlock. "What are you doing?"

His hands were staked above his head and his feet were also bound to the ground.

I continued my chant. I saw the fear in his eyes. It was real. His body convulsed in pain, and he let out a fierce scream.

I heard some of the coven gasp. "Don't stop your chant," Peggy screamed at them.

"Please stop, it hurts," Sam begged me, writhing in pain. He had no idea what was going on and I didn't have time to tell him.

Goddess of Earth I ask thee,
cleanse this man's soul from
the evil that holds him.
As I will it, so mote it be.

A white mist surrounded him, Sam's body convulsed again and his eyes watered. "No," he whispered.

A tear fell to my cheek. He thought I was trying to kill him.

I shook my head. "I love you, Sam."

I took the ceremonial knife and cut my palm. Dribbling the blood across his chest, I chanted.

He who is protected by my blood,
can hold no evil here.

Be gone.
As I will it, so mote it be.

The blood sizzled on his chest and burned like acid.

His eyes turned orange again. "You can't have him, bitch. I die, he goes with me." Blackstock's voice was a roar.

Bastard.

"No. You want real power. You want my power. Come on, I'll give it to you. Come to me, asshole. Let's play for real, stop hiding inside the warlock."

He rose above Sam as an orange mist. His form was that of the demon Blaseus, but I knew the voice.

The smell of sulfur was disgusting.

Hovering over Sam, he reached for me.

I threw the naming potion at him.

"I name you Blackstock and your soul belongs to the Blood Goddess." I moved to stand at Sam's head and poured half the Caiale down his throat. He choked and sputtered, but most of it went down.

I looked down. I couldn't see if he was breathing, but there was no time to check. If he lived, I hoped he'd forgive me. For now he had to die.

The mist rushed me and I drank the last of the Caiale.

The coven changed their chant, but Blackstock was so excited about possessing me he didn't notice.

Before I passed out I surrounded myself, and Sam, with a healing circle.

"Go to hell, asshole!" I screamed. My body convulsed and I fell to the ground.

I was dead, but I could see the coven, they continued the

chant, tears falling to their cheeks. Kira sobbing, but still repeating the words. I hovered above them.

Blackstock roared. He couldn't get out of our circle, and there was no one alive in the protected salt circle to possess. A demon can't possess a dead body. He looked up to the sky and then a giant mystical hand broke through the earth and pulled him into the ground.

Peggy broke the outside circle and poured the blue juice down Sam's throat and then mine.

The coven closed the circle behind her and continued their healing chant.

It's what kept Sam and me alive. I'm sure of it now.

I reentered my body gasping for air. Sam did the same. The circle broke and we cut the ties that bound Sam.

He reached for me. "God, I thought you were dead."

"I thought you were dead." I laughed. I should have been exhausted (almost dying usually does that to me) but I wasn't.

I touched his face. "I'm so sorry, I didn't know what else to do."

He squeezed me hard, his breath jagged.

Kira fell to her knees behind me and her arms circled us both. She sobbed. "I thought we were going to lose you both."

I laughed and cried. So did Sam. But these were tears of joy. We'd made it.

Everyone sat down on the ground. They'd been so powerful.

I held Sam but turned to them. "You were amazing."

Peggy smiled. "Girl, you sure do know how to stir up excitement around here. I don't know what we did for fun before you arrived." She said it jokingly, but I know she'd been affected by what had transpired tonight. We all had.

I later learned that Peggy and the coven had been watching the house. They felt Blackstock come through the instant he possessed Sam and made the calls to bring the coven in. I can't tell you how grateful I am these people have become my friends.

Sam is better than ever. We both slept about nine hours and he just went into town to pick up some food for dinner tonight.

His soul is lighter, as is mine. It's good to see him happy again. His strength amazes me.

Blackstock had been trying to possess him all this time, and Sam had been unknowingly fighting him. That's what had brought about all of those terrible insecurities, headaches and fevers.

Now that I know how bad he really felt, I'm even more amazed by Sam's abilities. He is a strong and gifted man.

I don't have long before he returns. I'm going to pick some flowers to put on the table.

Thirty

Tuesday, 2 P.M.
Sweet, Texas
Thoroughly happy witches with hot boyfriends: 1

I can barely walk, but it's worth it. Sam and I have been making love for the last forty-eight hours. We can't get enough of each other.

There's this new connection between us, even deeper than before. Oh, and he's so romantic.

Sunday, when he came back he had a lot more than food.

I was out in the conservatory repotting some of my herbs when he walked in carrying a beautiful rosebush. The roses were a deep red, almost black. Rich and velvety blooms.

"What's this?" I smiled.

He handed it to me. "I ordered it a while back, and had John open up the nursery so I could get it for you. It's called Red Witch, because of the enticing aroma. Kind of like *my* witch."

I laughed. "It's so beautiful, baby. Thank you." I moved it to the side so I could kiss him. His lips were so soft. Mmmm. I love the taste of Sam.

"Something else I've wanted to give you, but I've been waiting for the right time." He suddenly looked shy, and he stared at his shoes.

"What is it?" I thought it might be something from Victoria's Secret. The man has a thing for sexy lingerie that only rivals my own.

He took a deep breath.

"I love you, Bronwyn. You know that. More than anything. This last month, well it's been hell. For the first time ever, I wasn't sure I could go on. Not without you."

He shook his head before I could speak. "I know a lot of those insecurities had nothing to do with my own feelings and emotions. But the truth is, trusting is hard for me. And your job is so tough for me to take. That part of what I told you before was true, and straight from the heart. I can't stand the idea of losing you." His voice caught.

His eyes were so intense. I had no idea where he was going with this. Had he just given me a present and then he was breaking up with me? It didn't make any sense.

My emotions must have fallen across my face.

He laughed. "Stop it, baby, I'm trying to be romantic. I'm just not doing a very good job of it."

"Thank God." My whole body shook with giggles. "I wasn't sure what to think."

"Here." He held out his hand. A perfect Red Witch bloom

was in his hand. Draped on the rose was a beautiful silver necklace with a pendant.

"It's beautiful," I gasped. The pendant was shaped in two beautiful knots tied together.

He took it off the rose and walked behind me. Pushing my hair to the side, he placed it around my neck. "It's a Celtic eternal knot," he whispered against my ear. "This way I can be close to your heart at all times, even when you are thousands of miles away."

I turned to face him. He held my hands in his.

"I love you. I believe in you. And I'm so proud of you. I would never ask you to give up your job. But I do want you to be mine. Forever.

"I'm promising myself to you, Bron."

My arms flew around his neck.

"I love you so much." I kissed him all over his face and his neck and well, like I said, we've been in bed the last two days. He finally had to go into the office to see patients.

Oh, and I called Kira this morning. I remembered what Caleb had said about her hearing from the dead people that Blackstock was back.

"So, I guess you told Caleb." I was pruning out in the conservatory and had the phone cradled on my shoulder.

"Yes, and you were right. He took it really well." Kira laughed. "I almost got sick while I was trying to tell him, but he was so relieved that I wasn't seeing someone else. He said, considering the alternative, the dead people were a blessing."

So love is alive and well in Sweet, Texas.

And I'm in love with a gorgeous man who makes me happy. Yes, life is good.

Candace Havens is a veteran entertainment journalist who spends way too much time interviewing celebrities. In addition to her weekly columns seen in newspapers throughout the country, she is the entertainment critic for 96.3 KSCS in the Dallas/Fort Worth area. She is the author of *Charmed & Dangerous* and the non-fiction biography *Joss Whedon: The Genius Behind Buffy*, as well as several published essays. You can visit her at www.candacehavens.com or for the real crazy stuff at http://candyhavens.livejournal.com.